The Book of Unwritten Rules

Edited by Rufus Purdy

Paperback edition published by Studio 28, 28 Haymarket, London SW1Y 4SP.

ISBN: 978-1-78292-521-7

Contents

Introduction

The 14 writers who've created *The Book of Unwritten Rules* are a very special and very talented bunch of people. I, along with the author Christopher Wakling, was lucky enough to be their tutor on the Curtis Brown Creative Novel-Writing Course back in the Autumn of 2011 and, in the years since that three-month course ended, almost all have stayed closely in touch. Only one of the original 15 students has drifted away (though I'm sure she'd still be welcome to join up with the group again even now).

It was only Curtis Brown Creative's second-ever course, and the writing school was still something of a side project for me – a way of engaging more with new writers and nurturing talent (something that didn't feature strongly in my day job at the Curtis Brown literary agency). As a novelist who'd previously taught creative writing in a university setting, I thought we at Curtis Brown could run a fun, practical and innovative novel-writing school – free of all the bureaucratic rigmarole and academic red tape of the university context. I felt we could attract lots of talented writers, be selective about who we'd take on our courses and then use just a few short months to try to help them make their novels as good as possible and teach them some of the mysterious ways of the publishing industry with the input of successful novelists, our literary agents and leading publishers. The experiment worked rather better than I'd anticipated, and we now run a number of courses each year, both from our London offices and online, and – at the time of writing – 17 of our former students have gone on to get book deals with major publishers. But back to this little bunch…

Our most cohesive and sociable group ever, as well as one of the most talented, the students on our Autumn 2011 course were huge fun to teach. All were Real Writers and I knew straight away that some were writing novels that would find success. To date, four of the group have publishing deals: Tim Glencross, Kate Hamer, James Hannah and Annabelle Thorpe. They're hitting the bestseller lists and getting shortlisted for major prizes. And I have no doubt that more will follow.

Once the course ended, the group began to meet regularly, to read and discuss each other's novels in progress. And they have continued to run writing workshops, using exactly the format we'd used on the course. Sometimes they also just meet for a drink or two (they're a sociable bunch, as I've said). And it was at one of these meet-ups that they came up with the idea for *The Book of Unwritten Rules*.

During their novel-writing course, Christopher Wakling and I bombarded these poor people with rules: Show Don't Tell, Don't veer around between characters' heads mid-scene in your narrative perspective, don't open your book with someone waking up in the morning or staggering around with a hangover, etc, etc. These rules don't exist anywhere except in the ideas that we in the publishing industry have formed about what works and what doesn't – what readers do and don't like to encounter between the covers of a novel, and perhaps in creative-writing course folklore. Our students must get heartily sick of us laying down the law to them. Quite often, they decide to break those rules and, quite frankly, the rules exist to be broken. It's the experience of those unwritten rules, as delivered by the tutors and agents at Curtis Brown Creative, which has bound these 14 writers together. What a fabulous idea, then, to make it the unifying theme of this wonderful collection of stories.

In *The Book of Unwritten Rules* you'll encounter time travellers, suspicious wives, confused children, champagne thieves, stalkers, and so much more... It's a diverse and thoroughly delightful collection of stories from a diverse and thoroughly delightful group of writers. May this be the first of many such collections – and may you hear much more from these 14 writers.

Enjoy!

Anna Davis
Managing Director, Curtis Brown Creative, February 2016

The Delorean Travel Agency

Kate Bulpitt

These days when he met girls in pubs he told them he was a travel agent. Which he was, sort of.

There had been one last night. Blonde, pretty, but coated in foundation that Jaffa side of orange (weren't they all?), with eyelids laden down by lairy false lashes like mutant spiders' legs. He'd always gone for that sort, but now such lashes implied eyes-on-the-prize footballers' wives, not, as he'd recently realised, like in the Sixties, when they framed optimistic peepers seeing the swinging state of the nation. There was something about the new girls – or was that the old girls? – he was now meeting in his job that was so much more appealing than the easily impressed Jaffa lasses in Wetherspoons. Take her last night, whose eyes had widened when he told her what he did, the falsies impressively suspended, despite their weight.

He had a sought-after job. Each unit received hundreds of applications a week, both from aspiring Travel Associates and customers wanting to make bookings. There were plenty of those, and at the moment the average wait to take a trip was six months. Sometimes Johnny couldn't believe his luck. He knew to other people he seemed charming, a bit of a Jack the lad who'd always fall on his feet, but since college he'd been drifting, waiting for fate to intervene, liven things up. At school his cheeky charm carried him through – the women teachers would roll their eyes as he concluded his latest excuse for not handing in his homework, but with a smile and sunnily seduced, 'Oh Johnny, whatever are we going to do with you?', while the uniformed girls would follow him to the bike-sheds, gazing at him with teenage lust through rings of cigarette smoke.

Johnny had left school with few qualifications, so – not something he'd ever usually do – had faked them on his CV (he hadn't laid claim to the History or Psychology-related initials after his name that the job ad had requested, though once in the interview, he'd mention an education in psychology that didn't come with a certificate – the years spent in his Mum and Dad's pub. There was little human behaviour he hadn't seen there). He'd expected to be thrown out immediately, but after considering so many straight-laced academics, Seth enjoyed the bracing interruption of lively, unlikely Johnny.

Seth himself would never have had to fib about his academic achievements. He had a wunderkind brain fused for science, had taken A-levels at fourteen, finished a degree at sixteen, and – as was often quoted in numerous profiles about him – a childhood ingesting *Doctor Who*, *Back to the Future* and less likely suspect *Mr Benn* had started a deep-seated fascination with time travel. From the age of ten he'd been thinking quantum thoughts, tinkering with fantastical mathematical formulas. After decades of scientific speculation about parallel universes and time portals, two weeks before his fortieth birthday, Seth became the Quantum Physicist Who Could (champagne glass in hand and tongue in cheek, his mother implied it could have been much earlier that he achieved this success: 'The family dog, Smutty, went missing when Seth was fifteen. When I asked if he knew where Smutty could be, he always

8

said "He's gone to 1980"").

Keen that his work should make mankind's past accessible to anyone curious to experience it, Seth created The Delorean Travel Agency. Here ordinary souls could pay to visit (almost) any time and place in history (i). For an hour and twenty minutes (ii). Accompanied by an Agency Associate to ensure that nothing happened which might affect the space-time continuum (iii). (i) Except for each unit's one monthly Delorean Lottery winner, who receives a free trip, ensuring that not only those who can afford it get to travel; (ii) Maximum journey time, no exceptions; (iii) There are strict behavioural rules to be adhered to, and all Clients sign a contract underwritten by both national and international courts).

In Johnny's interview, Seth had asked, 'What makes you want to be part of our work?'

Johnny had considered this – possibly for the first time since he'd submitted his application. What had made him think he could, or should, travel through time? He'd never been that interested in the past – as a boy he'd liked robots and shiny new cars, as a teenager he'd thought the local *Quadrophenia*-watching mods were daft posers, and until recently, whenever he passed a vintage shop, he wondered why girls wanted to look like their grans. So why this, now? Was it something more than the coolest-sounding place to be between nights on the town, being able to tell girls in the pub that this was how he spent his days?

'Well,' he'd said eventually, looking Seth in the eye. 'I'd say it's the possibilities. I never felt there was much out there for me – you know, when you're fifteen you can see the next forty years ahead of you already: work, pub, girls... And there's nothing wrong with that, but it made me think of going into the unknown, I guess. I never thought of that before, I sort of thought the rest of my life was mapped out already.'

Seth liked Johnny – unassuming but confident, capable, curious. He could imagine people would feel in safe hands with him, at any point in time.

'We'll do a trial,' Seth said, 'Undertake an expedition, you and me, and if that goes well, then you've got a place here, we'll train you.'

For the trial they'd gone to 1988, the year Johnny was born. He'd wanted to laugh as Seth had handed him a pair of jeans with rips in them and a large, plain T-shirt.

'Fancy dress!' Johnny said.

'You need to fit in and look as inconspicuous as possible. Time-appropriate attire, but nothing too noticeable.' Seth passed Johnny a magazine and a tub of hair gel.

Johnny looked from one item to the other. The magazine was an issue of the old pop periodical, *Smash Hits*, and on the cover were a trio of sullen-looking lads with slicked-back hair.

'Blimey, look at the cheekbones on them!' said Johnny. 'Bet the girls loved 'em.'

Seth frowned. 'You did read the information pack you were sent?'

'Yep. And watched the disc.'

'Good. So were Bros not on there?'

'Aah,' Johnny tapped his forehead, 'Yeah! I forgot, sorry.' He started to hum a patchy line from one of the group's songs: 'When will I get my picture in the papers…?'

Johnny stood in front of a mirror, running gel through his hair while checking his efforts were enhancing his similarity to the pouting popsters. He almost laughed; this all seemed so incredible (if only his Mum and Dad could see him in this get-up – it was like one of the theme nights in the pub, when buxom middle-aged women would sing Bonnie Tyler songs on the karaoke and hit on Johnny as they ordered another round and told him to keep the change).

The trip itself had been awesome, in the actual sense of the word.

'We're not going to do anything remarkable,' Seth had said (which Johnny had found amusing and remarkable in itself), 'This is simply for you to begin to become acclimatised.'

They'd gone to the Travel Chamber, the reinforced steel door sliding shut behind them with a loud, confident click. Johnny had expected to be in awe of what he saw next, which was the Travel Unit itself. But at that point it just looked like the skeleton of a vehicle – the frame, the seats, the bulky boxes that contained the engine of sorts; something at the early end of a production line. Underwhelming, Johnny thought. Seth had climbed inside.

'Come on, then,' he'd said, beckoning Johnny to follow.

Johnny had taken a seat beside him. Seth entered some coordinates into a screen on the dashboard, setting their destination and also the form that the Travel Unit would take. There was whirring and clunking as the Unit's shell wrapped around them; in this case a blue, third-generation Ford Escort. Seth pressed another button and the Chamber's ExPort lights began to flash.

'Here we go,' he'd said, with a smile.

11

And so Johnny found himself sitting on a shopping precinct bench in June 1988, chatting nonchalantly with Seth as he tried to wrap his head around the fact that he was really there, and this wasn't some simulated reality, or effects of a particularly impressive hallucinogenic drug. The one external thing he could feel, which certainly seemed real, was the heat of the just-purchased Wimpy burger and chips that were in a paper bag currently warming his lap.

'Don't let those get cold,' said Seth.

Seth looked quietly impressed when a young guy with more rips in his jeans than he and Johnny combined walked past and, nodding in Johnny's direction, said:

'Hey man, looking good! Where'd you get your hair cut?'

Johnny had thought of himself with the tub of hair gel and *Smash Hits*, but with quick thinking and a smile said, 'My girlfriend does it for me.'

The guy grinned, gave a departing nod, and carried on by.

They wandered around some of the shops – checking out the latest electricals in Radio Rentals, flicking through car magazines in WH Smith – before Seth tapped his watch.

Now, months later, Johnny was really in the swing of things. A couple of weeks ago he'd been to London in 1964 to see The Beatles (all the Agency staff had seen them play, their shows being in the top three destinations – it had become a running joke, that the one trip every employee had in common was to the Cavern Club – to the point where they were running out of fresh staff faces to accompany their customers). The Client, Joyce, had wanted to stop in to a café close to the venue for a quick, calming cuppa.

She'd been too young to see the band at the time – had begged her parents, to no avail – and couldn't believe that now she had the chance.

'George was always my favourite,' she said, as they sat at a table near the door. She faced the window, watching the outside world; Johnny was opposite her looking in, marvelling at the prices on the board behind the counter (they'd been trained in pre-decimalisation notes and coins; to him, it was like holiday money).

'*Is* your favourite,' Johnny gently corrected her.

Joyce's eyes widened. 'Oh yes, sorry,' she whispered.

Johnny smiled reassuringly. He wasn't that bothered about seeing the Beatles again – though he would admit that it had been pretty electric the first time. He'd been more excited about getting to see the Prodigy at Glastonbury in 1995 a few weeks back. Guessing who else might be on their way to the show, he glanced discreetly around the room. This casual survey stopped as soon as he saw her: a woman in a pale-green coat, stirring sugar into a teacup, seemingly lost in thought – glancing down towards the table with a coy smile on her face, as though she had a secret in mind that Johnny instantly wanted her to share. He was mesmerised, hypnotised by the swirl of her delicate wrist as she spun the spoon slowly around. She must have sensed it because she looked up, directly at him, and even though he knew they'd been instructed to keep any interactions to a minimum, that he was supposed to avoid eye contact, to look away (this was capitalised in the Rule Book), he was transfixed. Love at first sight. She smiled, then turned back to her cup, taking the spoon and resting it gently on the saucer.

'Shall we go?' said Joyce, with a shiver of excitement. Johnny had shivered too.

* * *

Molly glanced at her calendar. Her next appointment was in ten minutes, with a woman whose initial application stated that she wished to travel to the very festive Festival of Britain. This had been given to Molly as she'd already been to that once, so would have some familiarity (though repeated trips to the same time or place were controlled carefully, so as not to create recognition amongst the Originals there).

Every day here was a dream for Molly. She would never have thought, as she pored over history books, biographies and historical novels, trotted, wonder-struck, around museums and stately homes, and dedicated herself – at the expense of much social merriment – to achieving a First Class History degree at a Cambridge college, that she could use her knowledge for this. That she had unwittingly prepared herself for the greatest job she could ever have imagined (and actually, she would never have imagined such an outlandish thing).

Just this week, her most memorable experience had been in a tea room in 1912, where she overheard a woman proudly telling a friend that her son had bought a ticket for the *Titanic*, and was off to try his fortunes in America. Molly had thought of turning and telling the mother to beg him to stay, but knew she could not interfere. Instead she crossed her fingers and hoped he would be one of the few to make it. She'd danced in the streets on VE Day, and in 1953 lined Pall Mall as the Queen's coach sped past after the Coronation. But more often than not it wasn't big events that people wanted to relive, they wanted to walk down the street where they grew up, to visit childhood holiday locales, to experience times and places described by their parents and grandparents. She knew that as well as anyone. So far her favourite moment, silly as it seemed, was in the 1960s, walking past the London dancehall where her parents met. She'd almost feigned needing the loo so she could hop in and see inside, but given how little time the Client had for their visit, it would have been wholly unfair to take up a few precious minutes, and she wasn't allowed to leave anyone alone while they were away.

In front of her, a woman in a feather-adorned hat cleared her throat.

'My husband has a friend who's filled out an application, can I leave that here?'

'Yes, I can take that,' Molly said, as the woman fished in her bag for the form.

Molly glanced over it. 'I'm sorry, we can't accept this. There are restrictions on visiting Germany in 1939.'

'But it doesn't say–'

'I know, but there are certain places we just can't allow visits to, for obvious reasons. The world and their milkman wants to kill Hitler, stop John Lennon being shot, work out what really happened on the grassy knoll...' Molly smiled gently, 'You'll have to tell him it's a no, I'm afraid.'

There were more rules, and plenty of them. You could only travel back, not forwards. Morally Seth didn't want to play God with anyone seeing their future, plus, it seemed dangerous for anyone to see developments and technologies before they'd occurred. There were no exceptions to the hour and twenty minute journey time; when asked why, Seth would simply say that visiting time had to be limited, and he liked the number 80 – 'Not quite enough time to cause trouble, I hope.' Travel to war zones or unstable times was not permitted. You weren't allowed to visit anywhere where you might bump into your younger self or any relatives. If you weren't alive during the time you were visiting, or were too young to remember it, you were given a detailed information pack, which you had to read in one of the Agency's research booths – and there was a short test afterwards. Cross-company schedules were carefully coordinated so that there were never more than six travellers loose in the past at any one time. Absolutely no photographic souvenirs were permitted, and Clients were advised in no uncertain terms to avoid any cameras or filming equipment when travelling. Visits to any period before the 1940s were more expensive than later dates, involving considerably more Client training and an escort with specialist knowledge. The same applied to foreign travel. Initially they only booked appointments to gad within the UK, but as the team of experts grew, that had expanded to include other parts of Europe, and some worldwide places, depending on which branch you went to (Hilary in the Edinburgh Agency was very knowledgeable about Ancient Rome and keen to lead visits there, but there were still concerns as to how folk from the present would be able to bob about there unnoticed. 'Ah Seth,' she'd say, 'Can't you invent some wee invisibility cloaks?').

Molly leant back in her chair, considering for a moment – again – about how what they were doing, even though they were extraordinarily careful, might be affecting the past. Could they really dip in and out without causing any effect? That this travel was possible was beyond incredible. When she stopped to think about it, about how she now spent hours of her time, it boggled her mind. Like thinking of infinity. Seth had explained it to her, many times, how he had made it so. 'Tell me again,' she'd sometimes say (worrying he'd think she was a simpleton, but she couldn't help herself), and he would, as though it was her most beloved bedtime story.

There was a bleep on her screen and Seth's face appeared, in a video link. He was wearing a shirt covered in small elephants. He loved animal prints.

'Hello, you,' said Molly, with a giddy smile.

'Hi, Moll,' he replied, with an adorably geeky wave and as giddy a smile as he tended to muster. 'How goes your day?'

'All the better for seeing you. But in other news, I've just finished a psych assessment on a lady who's going to Florence in 1981 – holiday romance-related, I'd say, so a bit tricky – turned down an application to Berlin in 1939–'

Seth tutted.

'And this afternoon I'm gadding to 1974 to see Abba win Eurovision.'

'Really?'

'Yes, with a lovely guy who remembers watching it with his Mum on telly before she died. They had cake and drank snowballs, and he ended the evening by telling her he was gay. She said, "Of

17

course you are, love, and it makes no difference to me." It's going to be emotional.'

'So he really would have liked to have watched it with his Mum again...'

Molly sighed, 'Yes, but what can we do.' With a small laugh, she added, 'Until you can invent those invisibility cloaks...'

'Ah, I wish. I'm not that brilliant.'

'I think you are.'

Molly still had to pinch herself sometimes, to think Seth, the genius, the revolutionary, could like her. There had been an attraction as soon as they met. They'd both spent their formative years absorbed by studies, both been to Cambridge, both owned DVDs of *Mr Benn*. In her interview, Seth had asked the top three places she'd most like to quantum visit, and she'd said the court of Elizabeth I, a Suffragette march, and the London dancehall where her Mum and Dad had met in the 1960s. At that mention of the Silver Palace, Seth's jaw had dropped.

'My parents met there, too,' he'd said, his eyebrows knitting suddenly in an almost subdued, frowning concentration, as though mentally calculating the statistical likelihood of this remarkable coincidence. Then he'd smiled, and pointed out a black-and-white photo on his desk – his mother, at a party, glass of wine in hand, smiling at something out of frame. She was exceptionally pretty, her hair swept into a modest beehive, and wearing a simple, close-fitting dark dress adorned with a diamanté deer brooch, which reminded Molly of Babycham bottles.

Molly had excelled at her Agency training, naturally, and Seth had asked her to dinner the night that she completed it. They'd been together ever since.

'Are you still okay for supper tomorrow?' he asked, on the video link. 'Want to come to mine?'

'Definitely.'

Seth cleared his throat and said, 'I've got a surprise for you.'

'Oh! A nice one?'

Seth gave a nervous smile. 'I hope so.' His phone rang, and he glanced across at it. 'Ah, sorry. I should go.'

They said their goodbyes. Molly left her desk and went through to the Changing Rooms. Here they would select era-appropriate outfits for they and their Client to wear. It was much easier to pick clothes for Clients in advance, otherwise they'd become so distracted by the options that they'd be late for the travel slot itself. Molly checked her schedule; April 1974, weather: cloudy. Noting the Client's sizes, she gathered for him a pair of dark-blue flared trousers, a cream shirt, and a mac. In a manila folder were the info pack (which would be left here at the office) and a pair of carefully created tickets for the Eurovision venue, printed on edible, swiftly biodegrading paper which, if they didn't get to ingest, or if any pieces were left behind, would, as Seth liked to say 'self-destruct'. Nothing was left to chance.

An alarm began to sound, like the bringing bell of an old telephone, but with a single, stilted ring, and Molly glanced towards the ImPorting sign, lit up on the wall, now flashing amber. Someone had just got back. The Client would be immediately transferred to the Debrief room (where a normalising cup of decaffeinated tea would await them) to discuss their experience and how they were feeling; it could take hours before they were ready to go home, and days, sometimes weeks, to get over the shock, excitement and disbelief of their trip. Molly had yet to meet anyone who didn't want to go again, or to stay longer, and despite the psychological assessment, it was impossible to prepare anyone for life after time travel. To call it moreish would be an understatement; this could be the most extraordinary, mind-bending high a person could experience.

* * *

The Eurovision excursion proved to be as uplifting, emotional and bonkers as Molly had anticipated. It was the end of the day, and she sat quietly on a sofa in one of the Debrief rooms, drinking elderflower cordial and decompressing. Johnny leant into the room; they were last to leave.

'Fun day?'

Molly nodded. 'Barmy, isn't it? You almost think it hasn't, and then–'

'It blows your mind every time.'

Molly smiled. Her ears were still ringing with 'Waterloo'.

'The other day I thought I met the woman of my dreams. I got back and thought – did that just happen, or didn't it? Sometimes I still don't get if it means the trips we take become part of what happened, or they don't.'

'It certainly tests the brain.' There was a pause. 'Where were you? When you saw her?'

'1964, on my way to see the Beatles.'

They both laughed.

'Been there, done that…' said Molly.

'Weren't allowed to buy the T-shirt.'

'I passed the Soho nightclub where my parents met. I so wanted to go in. If only we got to pick the trips.'

Johnny looked thoughtful, then a flash of mischief crossed his face.

'Why don't we go? Now? Just for half an hour.'

Molly's wistful expression turned serious. 'No,' she shook her head, 'No way, we can't. Absolutely not.'

'Come on, we're pros. What harm can it do? I check out the ladies, you see the club, we come back–'

'Nice idea, but no.'

Johnny turned the charm dial up a notch or two. 'Ah, go on. What's the difference in us going now, and the rest of the trips we take? All the units are closed, we're not going to clash with anyone.' He turned on his best megawatt puppy smile.

'Seth would be furious.'

'Why? We're not going to kill Hitler. When else will you get to see inside the club? Not when you go for work,' Johnny cajoled, 'there's never time to do anything besides what the customers want. And I bet it's amazing.'

Molly had hoped that she and Seth might go one day – a date, to see where their parents had met – but he himself didn't like to travel. Obviously he had done, early on, but now he said he preferred to leave it to others – and to be on hand, in the present, in case of any problems that he might need to step in and fix.

Johnny added one more notch, for good measure. 'Well, I'm heading to the Changing Room. Then I'm going, so if you don't come, there'll be no-one to keep an eye on me.'

Fifteen minutes later they were on their way. Molly pushed aside her doubts and concentrated on the excitement. She was going to the Silver Palace!

As they stepped onto the street, Johnny murmured, 'I wonder if she's thought about me.'

'Who?' Molly asked, distracted, wondering if she might have a cocktail.

'The girl. From the other day.'

Molly turned to him, feeling uneasy. She'd thought he was just here on a spontaneous, naughty jaunt. 'Oh Johnny, you need to be careful, you can't think like that.'

Johnny winked in response.

The Silver Palace was as breathtaking as Molly had wanted it to be, sporting a now fading '50s grandeur, which she found utterly charming. It was smaller than she'd thought, but that only made it more intimate. Now she felt as the earlier client, Eric, had at Eurovision, and she excused herself to go and powder her nose.

When she returned, she made her way round the edge of the room, beside the tables, careful not to make eye contact with anyone. Now she was here, she began to worry that she might bump into her Mum and Dad (she knew they hadn't met until 1969, but still). She glanced down at her pointy black shoes, stepping on the curls of the rich, rouge swirly carpet. Then, looking back up, Molly noticed Johnny at the bar, talking to a woman – she was realising now what a caution he was with the ladies. Johnny's back was to her, and as Molly approached, she got a closer view of the woman. Shiny, beehived hair, wide eyes with heavy lashes, and pink lips that she licked distractedly, head tilted, as she listened to Johnny's small talk. She almost looked familiar, in the odd way that people in the past sometimes did. And then Molly saw her brooch – a diamanté deer. She blinked, surprised, and looked away, wondering if refocussing – like shaking an etch-a-sketch – would clear the image. But she looked again, and there it was. Molly moved towards Johnny, willing him to catch her eye. Now with the barman's attention, the woman turned briefly away.

Wide-eyed, Johnny mouthed, 'It's her!'

'You can't talk to her,' Molly whispered, trying to mask her fright with quiet authority.

'I know… but she's the one!' he whispered eagerly, 'What are the chances?'

Molly grasped his arm and stared him straight in the eye. 'Johnny, I'm fairly certain that's Seth's mother.'

His face wrinkled in confusion. 'It can't be.'

'Yes, it can, and we really need to leave.'

'But I– What if she's–'

'What? Nothing can happen with anyone here, least of all her. We need to go.'

Johnny looked at the woman; he was more doe-eyed than the diamanté deer. What if he didn't meet someone like her again? What if he was supposed to be here? In this swinging land of beautiful girls and Beatles gigs that not long ago he'd only seen in black-and-white clips on the telly, but which was now a world of glorious Technicolor. How could he return to fake tan and Saturday nights getting ready in front of telly talent shows when there was this?

23

Behind him, Molly was clutching his arm so tightly he thought she might stop his circulation. She had never wanted to be back in the present more badly. She thought of Seth, now wishing more than anything that she could forget time travel and be at home with him. What was I thinking? she wondered. How did we think we'd get away with this? It had been a terrible idea, but if Johnny couldn't put a pin in his infatuation things could get substantially worse. The only man who this young woman needed to become entangled with was Seth's Dad, and any deviation might mean... Molly shuddered.

The woman turned back, gave Johnny a keen smile. 'So, you didn't tell me,' she said, 'What do you do?'

Johnny gazed at her. Could he leave? Could he stay?

He cleared his throat. 'Funny you should ask, I'm a travel agent, sort of. You wouldn't believe some of the places I've been...'

Ugly

Julie Nuernberg

Phase 1

He needs to have blonde hair, blue eyes, a strong jawline and good cheekbones. He needs to be amazingly attractive – and I mean the level of attractiveness where average-looking people stop in their tracks, mouths open, staring, wishing. Head-to-toe perfection; like me. I'm getting impatient. I can't find him. I flip through the three-ring binders with laminated descriptions of the donors. Harvard-educated. Neurophysicist. Blah, blah. Who cares if you're smart? I don't have a degree from an Ivy League school and it didn't stop me from being Mr Thompson's executive assistant. *The* Mr Thompson, who runs the biggest timeshare business in southwest Florida. He's old, nearly 5-0, but he looks 35. He's got a full head of dyed hair and gets regular Botox, and that's why he is the successful businessman that he is. We're two of a kind, we're extraordinarily good-looking people and that's why we've achieved what we've achieved. And my baby is going to be jaw-dropping gorgeous – I am going to make sure it has the same opportunities as me.

I turn the page to some premature balding guy with a nose that is too wide across the base and a depressing lack of cheekbones, who went to MIT. Like that makes up for it. It's soul-destroying. I sigh and push my hair into a high ponytail. I look good with a ponytail, especially when I walk; I make it swish back and forth, like a racehorse. I keep flipping the pages until there HE is. He looks like a Ken doll, plastic fantastic with a chiselled face, bright blue eyes, no sign of a receding hairline. I scan down to his hobbies; working out. That's it, just working out. Simple and straightforward. His education shows he graduated high school. He doesn't try to make up for any lack in beauty with education, because he doesn't need to. He is perfect, he is the one. Number 5436 – you and me are going to have a beautiful baby.

It was about a year ago that I decided I wanted a kid. I had been feeling kind of empty inside and it came to me one night. I had this urge to see myself in another human being. I wanted to stand next to my creation and we'd smile in the mirror together and we'd look the same and it would be amazing. And how adorable would it be to dress up in coordinating outfits and go for a walk where people would stop us to tell us how cute we are? But there couldn't be a daddy in this picture. I knew I had to do this on my own. I wanted this baby to be all mine. I didn't want some guy telling me how to do the kid's hair, what shoes she had to wear. He would take away all my fun. No, this is why I am going solo. I'm not telling anyone, not even my mother. It's pointless, she would never understand. The conversation would go something like this:

'I forbid it. You'll ruin your body. And we've worked so hard.'

'Hello? Isn't that what plastic surgery is for? Haven't you taught me that anything is possible under the knife?'

'You know that there are limits to what doctors can do. And I have never been able to fix what you did to me. If I could do it all over again…'

Do I need to go on?

Phase 2

Eight months down the line, 5436's insemination is a big success. And I look amazing in little summer maternity dresses. To be honest, when the test came back positive, my mother's fears did make me second-guess myself. There are some real stunners out there who have just fallen apart at the seams from pregnancy. I cried for Jessica Simpson when I saw the pictures in *People* magazine. How awful that must have been for her. And Kim Kardashian – oh the horror. Those sausage feet and massive boobs! I don't care how much udder balm she slathered on each day, she's going to be covered in stretch marks.

Some ladies get a glow. Thankfully that's me and then some. The other girls in the office tell me I don't even look pregnant, which makes me so happy. I still see Mr Thompson checking me out when I bring in his morning coffee and low-fat muffin. Not in a pervy way (we have the utmost respect for each other), but more like a dad looking approvingly at his incredibly hot daughter. Like Joe Simpson did to Jessica – pre-pregnancy of course. And I think it's all because I've been watching my weight; that's the secret. I still eat my same diet every day, fresh fruit for breakfast, tuna salad for lunch and chicken breast for dinner. My mother, once she started talking to me again, said she only put on 10lbs with me. 'Less to take off after,' she whispered.

Phase 3

I'm at my final check-up. My doctor is making me have an ultrasound again and I'm not a fan of the cold jelly on my stomach – it is extremely drying to the skin. But it doesn't matter; I'm so excited because the hospital is right by this little boutique that has the cutest baby clothing. I don't know what I'm having. I love surprises. So I've been buying the most gorgeous little sailor suits and party dresses. Whatever it is, it will be well-dressed.

I'm tying my hospital gown tighter to give me a more defined waist when my doctor comes in. He is handsome, I made sure of that, but a lower-lid blepharoplasty would do wonders for him. I start to tell him this, but he interrupts me.

'I'm sorry to have to tell you that your baby is in trouble.'

'Oh God.' My heart starts pounding. What a waste this will be if I don't have a kid.

'The heartbeat is weak and the baby is struggling. We're going to need to do an emergency Caesarean section today.'

'OK, whatever you think is best.'

This is brilliant news! I was so worried that I would tear and the doctor wouldn't sew me up properly, not to mention the damage a natural birth would do to my pelvic floor muscles. Peeing every time I laugh or sneeze for the rest of my life? No thank you. I had been doing so many Kegel exercises in preparation that I was doing them in my sleep, but there's no guarantee that the muscles won't be weakened. I feel a Caesarean is a very good sign.

I am wheeled into the operating room and I fan my hair around me on the pillow. I want to look good when my baby sees me for the first time. It's all very fast. Everyone seems to be quite panicked and racing about; metal instruments banging on trays. I tune it all out and think positive thoughts that the scar will be minimal. With the baby so small, surely they don't need to make too wide an opening. The nurses and doctor are gathered around my stomach and they have put up a sheet as a barrier, which is OK with me. I recognise the nurse who was there when I had my irises made a shade called 'distinctively denim'. And I smile and give her a small wave, but she just stares at me. Then the doctor is shouting 'yes, yes' and then there is crying. A horrible cry. It sounds like a cat is being strangled. The doctor holds the baby high so I can see, but it has its head turned to the side so I can't get a good look. They whisk it away and fuss over it for some time while the doctor keeps working on me. I visualise words like small, invisible, tight. Then it's back, wrapped in a blanket and they place it on my chest.

'A healthy baby girl!'

'She looks just like her mother.'

I examine her closely; she looks nothing like me. She's the opposite. No hair, flat nose, squinty eyes, short arms and legs. Vomit rises in my throat and I gag. Someone grabs the baby, a nurse runs over with a pan and I'm sick. I try to catch them, but the tips of my hair drop into the yellow bile, and I shudder and vomit again.

'The anaesthetic will do that. Don't worry, it's normal to be queasy.' The nurse is holding the baby and I can see its profile with its bulging forehead and recessed chin.

'Get that thing away from me!'

I lay back and a nurse puts the baby on my chest again. I don't want it there, I don't want it anywhere near me. The baby keeps crying. This god-awful screeching. I look at its mouth, not open in a sweet, round 'O', but a lopsided shape, all red gums, lips curled back. And I start to cry, too, but soft tears that I know stream down my cheeks gracefully. There must be a mistake. Maybe they didn't give me 5436's sperm. I gasp. What if they gave me one of those ugly guys' sperm? What if this thing stays ugly all its life? I hand the baby back to a nurse.

'Take it away and get me my mother… I'm going to faint now.' And everything goes black.

I wake up back in my hospital room. For a minute, I feel relief; it's all been a horrible nightmare. I'm still pregnant and I'm going to have the most beautiful baby. I smile and turn to see my mother sitting next to my bed. I see by her face it is real. She's been crying but I can only tell this by a small sniffle and the handkerchief that she dabs at her eyes. She's had her hair done. It looks lovely in a layered cut and I can see she's had some honey highlights added to her golden colour.

'I told you not to do this. But you had to, you just had to.' She balls the handkerchief in her hand.

'Did you even go see it?'

'Yes, of course, why do you think I'm so furious with you? What have you done?'

I start to cry. I want her to be supportive. I wish she'd say she'll help me and we'll get through it. I want my mother to say it. I want her to admit the baby is hideous. That I have given birth to a monster. And that we'll fix it.

'Just say it mother. She's ugly. She's the ugliest kid that's ever been born and I'm suing that fucking clinic because they have messed up. They've given me someone else's sperm. Her donor was gorgeous – there is no way in hell that our genes made that. No way.' I feel the pain of my incision and I curse that kid for what it has done to me.

My mother shakes her head and weeps, her head bent down, the lovely layering cascading forward.

'Don't you ever wonder why there's no baby pictures of you? You just had to be greedy, didn't you? You just couldn't be happy with what you've got!'

She sweeps out the room and Chanel No.5 breezes over my face. I breathe it in deeply. I don't even get a chance to think about what she means by being greedy and no baby pictures because the nurse brings in the kid and says I have to try to feed. She shows me how to hold the monster and pulls down my gown so my breast is exposed. I know I look good like this, with the exception of the baby. If my mother was still here, I'd have her take a picture then I'd Photoshop the kid right out of it. The nurse is happy because the beast latches on after only a couple of tries. She leaves me alone and I stare at it as it sucks furiously, making gross slurping sounds and I imagine my breast deflating, a sad saggy sack of skin remaining after this kid sucks me dry just so it can grow to be a fatty. Now that's greedy! I waver between thoughts of smothering it and putting it up for adoption.

The next few days are a blur. I try to get my head around what has happened. Girlfriends come to visit with balloons and flowers and stuffed animals. And with everyone it's the same. They say, 'Aren't you lucky? A healthy baby girl.' Not at any time are the words pretty, beautiful, cute, adorable, stunning used. One girlfriend who has always been jealous of me says, 'she has your mouth.' She looks delighted.

Mr Thompson drops in, too, and I know he likes that I've straightened my hair and I'm wearing a pink headband. I feel I need to work that much harder to compensate for what I've produced. He leans over the bassinet and I see his smile tighten for just a split second. I've got a lifetime to deal with this. Disappointment. Beauty should produce beauty. It's the law of nature. He doesn't say anything, but just comes over and squeezes my hand. I feel tears welling and my bottom lip quivers in spite of the fillers.

'Now, now. There's no need for that. This isn't forever. You have access to the best plastic surgeons here in Florida. You can make her as beautiful as you.'

Like everyone else, Mr Thompson makes a fast exit and I stare into my compact mirror, slowly applying lipgloss as the baby cries next to me. His words go round and round in my head and I feel stronger, I feel hopeful. He is right. I can make her into the beautiful girl I want her to be. But then I think of Tori Spelling and know that plastic surgeons can only do so much.

My mother picks me up when I'm discharged. I tell her we'll take the kid to a plastic surgeon as soon as we can; that we can turn this around.

'No, you've got to give them something solid to work with. We need to do it ourselves then the surgeons can complete the work when she's 16.'

I'm not sure what she means, but I breathe a sigh of relief. I am so happy this isn't just my problem anymore.

Phase 4

I name her Bella. I believe in positive thinking. Every time I say her name it is bringing to life the goal we are working towards. I go back to work after six weeks, back into my pre-pregnancy clothes and a rumour starts around the office that I never even had a baby. I don't put a picture on my desk of Bella. I don't post on Facebook about her. I don't mention her to anyone. But she is all I think about. When Mr Thompson is out at meetings, I read online about soft cartilage, how bone grows. And, at night, my mother shows me how to make masks and splints, how to elongate the arms and legs, how to take advantage of the unfused plates in her cranium. I limit her intake of calcium so her bones stay soft for longer, longer for me to work. My mother watches Bella while I'm at the office and monitors her pain relief so she isn't screaming all the time; and, most importantly, she makes sure that Bella doesn't pull off the contraptions taped to her face. Each night we take precise, time-consuming measurements and document them along with close-up and full-body photos of Bella. I never pose with her in these pictures, but I look forward to the day when I can.

Phase 5

It is hard work but it's all worth it. When Bella turns six, she cannot read or count, BUT she is no longer the hideous creature that came out of my toned tummy. Her nose is pert, a straight slope to an upturned tip. Her face is oval-shaped, like mine; not the square she was born with. That was probably the most difficult task, getting her boxy chin to go into a smooth point. I dye her mousy brown hair blonde on the first Sunday of each month. And, after much research, I find an eye doctor who works on film sets to create blue lenses for her, making new ones every few months as her eyes grow. He matches them to my own denim-blue and tells me I have magnificent eyes and everyone should have my colour. I nod in agreement.

While some kids merely play with Barbie, Bella worships Barbie. She does yoga and Pilates for two hours each morning to make her limbs long and lean. And she does not complain. Bella knows nothing else but making herself beautiful and she understands that there must be pain involved. She can't tell you a Dr Seuss story but she can quote our role model Kate Moss, 'nothing tastes as good as skinny feels'. Such wise words. Her education is my imparted knowledge of exercise, nutrition, fillers, Botox, implants and what I think works best, and she soaks it up like a sponge. We are working towards the day when Bella can meet the world. And on that day, we'll wake up early before the sun rises and I'll wash, set and style our hair, backcombing so we have ample volume. I'll put make-up on us: mascara, eyeliner, lip plumper with a berry hue. We'll each wear a blue fitted dress that matches our blue eyes. When I am finished, I'll make Bella stand with me in front of the mirror. We'll stay there for ages, poising and pouting. And there will be so much beauty I won't be able to stand it.

Look and Assess

James Hannah

I found myself, this afternoon, sitting in an otherwise empty X-ray department waiting room, awaiting an X-ray for my suspected broken rib. It is, like just about every hospital department I've been to, the domain of capable women. Mothers of the NHS, the women who can.

But these women, long on efficiency, long on practicality – long on care, even – fall decidedly short on patience. They've transformed the reception and the waiting room into what I can only say is an ad hoc gallery dedicated to their unwillingness to fulfil even the most rudimentary requirements of communication with the poor old buggers like me who stump unwittingly up the corridor.

Sitting on my own, awaiting my appointment, I noticed that the regulation NHS blue-and-white plastic sign on the door of the staff toilet (reading 'Staff Toilet') had been embellished with a notice printed on A4 in a jaunty comic script: 'This is NOT a public toilet'. The word 'NOT' all in capitals and further enhanced with fluorescent marker (now faded).

Behind me, another factual notice ('X-ray results will not be given today, but will be delivered to your GP') was also backed up with the more emotional – and, this time, laminated – printout: 'Take responsibility for collecting your X-ray's from your GP'. Feeling a little chastised, I was struck by the matronising tone. *For the love of God just take some responsibility!*

And good heavens, it was like being back at St Leonard's Terrace again, the fridge front packed full of Post-It notes, an actual heavens-to-Betsy checklist on the inside of the cupboard door, headed Things To Do Before Your Dram. I can still reel them off even now. 'Shirt in the linen bin, washing up, drying up *and* putting away, rotate the fresh veg.'

Rotate the fresh veg.

And all of this is lieu of a conversation, in lieu of a relationship. In lieu of respect.

I won't have these things said to me.

This is people's lives – this is *my* life – these women are dealing with, for heaven's sake. My dignity. It is not – it simply is *not* – good enough to print out and stick up a sign, rather than personally ensure adequate communication has been achieved. Let me say this, if I say nothing else: we live in a post-convenience world. Some of us, on occasion, will actively have to get up off our big backsides and do something. We can't all sit there, idly playing solitaire.

Alone though I was in that waiting room, it was with a little fraternal thrill that I noticed some past patient had, in a modest attempt at rebellion, taken the trouble of circling the greengrocer's apostrophe that appeared on the word 'X-ray's'; the blue biro, alas, inadequately marking the laminate.

This act of quiet defiance pleased me, because I myself had been considering how I might surreptitiously amend 'This is NOT a public toilet', by crossing through all the words and replacing them with the far more useful 'Nearest public toilet down the corridor, second left'. Just – and this is merely a suggestion – a small tonal adjustment with a judicious sprinkling of fact to prevent the patients from feeling humiliated for just wishing to answer nature's call.

However, the frustration inherent in these little notices was reduced to its most perfect form when finally I was called in for my X-ray. On the inside of the heavy lead door of the X-ray room itself, I noticed a small grubby sticker at eye-height, making the following exhortation: 'PULL'.

I couldn't help but imagine the sequence of events that will have led to that sticker being stuck there. I considered the synaptical adjustment that goes on in an outpatient's head when they've just pushed a pull door. Multiply that by the number of outpatients who must troop through that doorway each day. Imagine the resentment that must build up in you if you're the poor X-ray attendant who has to not only see but *anticipate* every single outpatient on your list doing the same thing – *they're going to push the door, I just know they're going to push it!… Gah!*

Indulge me a moment: All of this brings to mind the time last summer when – what was her name? – Abigail: Abigail and I met on the corner by the old cinema, and made our way to Spritzy's Wine Bar on Tipton Street.

Here's what happened: we went in, and Abigail wasn't keen, so we came out. Then we realised there was really nowhere else to go within walking distance – at least in those shoes – so we went back in again and had a drink, before leaving relatively early on account of her recently remembered appointment the following morning.

All well and good. But between the bartender and the rainsprung pavement of Tipton Street was a single set of double doors. Just one. And as is increasingly the case, I find, only one of the doors was unlocked. Something to do with the air conditioning, perhaps, I don't know. We passed through those doors on four occasions (in, out, in, out), and – I could blame myself for this, but it was a simple act of old-fashioned chivalry – Abigail led the way through the doors on all four journeys.

The sequence I endured was as follows:

1. In: push the locked door; pull the locked door; push the unlocked door; pull the unlocked door open and through.
2. Out: pull the locked door; push the locked door; pull the unlocked door; push the unlocked door open and through.
3. In: push the locked door; pull the locked door; push the unlocked door; pull the unlocked door open and through.
4. Out: pull the locked door; push the locked door; pull the unlocked door…

It was at this moment that I snapped, and history records that I shouted: 'LOOK AND ASSESS!'

Well now it has become apparent to me that one of the things I do unconsciously as I approach a set of double doors is to look at the shape of the joinery and where the doorstops are situated, and conclude which door is likely to be unlocked, and which way it might go. I flatter myself I almost always pass through unchecked. It turns out that most of the population don't avail themselves of this simple precaution. They, I am informed, haven't the time for such an anally retentive way of living their day-to-day existences.

So I understand the frustration of those hospital sign-writers, I genuinely do.

But it was the *tone* of these notices that left me feeling prejudged. The world, these women have clearly concluded, is full of idiots.

So, I was sitting there awaiting the confirmation of my X-ray, and feeling at a low ebb with regard to humanity, when finally humanity was restored to me in just the smallest of ways. The X-ray attendant said: 'You're free to go now; the results will be available from your GP in about ten days.' That's right, she accepted that, even if there is a sign telling you precisely that, sometimes it is good to take the responsibility of *speaking it out loud*.

'Yes,' I said, appreciatively, 'I understand that. I'll be sure to make an appointment.' I had read and absorbed the sign outside. Tick.

I picked up my bag and coat, and pushed the door.

I pulled the door.

Smoke and Mirrors

Julia Armfield

Once upon a time, there were four magicians.
Well, one or four, depending on your outlook.

* * *

'The surprising fact about your audience,' as Harold always used to say, 'is that they want to be fooled, probably more than you want to fool them. Now that's not to say that any self-respecting audience member is just going to look the other way when you've got cards sticking out of your cuffs or bent spoons in your pockets, but it does mean that if you're *good*, they'll generally allow themselves to be convinced of something they know is bullshit for as long as you need them to be.'

He had never been a natural at cursing. His whole body would coil in around the word before letting it out, hands flying and eyes snapping as though forcibly ejecting something bad. He liked to eat apples during lectures, and these almost always ended up sailing merrily away to some distant corner of the room when his arms flailed too hard, leaving him always mildly surprised and with juice trickling backwards down his wrists.

Leo liked to say it was rather like being taught the secrets of the universe by someone he'd got stuck sitting next to on a bus – a statement he would usually bring out tilted back on two legs of a desk chair and shuffling tarot cards with his little finger sticking out.

'He's a genius,' Magnus would reply, starchy-faced and unlaughing, and Leo would twirl his cards back and forth between his knuckles, holding up the Death card with teasing teeth hooking forwards over his lips.

The apples, incidentally, were seldom rescued from the darker reaches of the room, but rather generally left to stew beneath chairs and in the grate of the empty fireplace, with the result that the room always smelled like bad jam and ammonia; an odour which clung to curtains and carpets and the insides of your clothes.

* * *

The Academy was just something they called it to make it sound less like what it actually was; three young magicians learning card tricks from an old one at his house in Bethnal Green. He had been, so they heard, one of the great Music Hall magicians and a friend to Arthur Askey and Gus Elen. But his house spoke more of damp than it did of former glories and many was the time, coming out of the second-floor bathroom, that one of them would find themselves stuck with a foot through the floorboards that tended to give wherever there was plumbing nearby. (This was all very well for Magnus who, after all, wanted to be an escapologist, but for the others it was frankly just a pain.)

It was a house of sudden skylights and treacherous stairs, blind corners piled high with packing cases, spider plants potted in hat boxes, glove puppets slung over the beds. On every floor was some testament to Harold's old career – top hats, kid gloves, trick mirrors, magic boxes, a white rabbit stuffed and mounted on top of the TV. Roxanne said it reminded her of the kind of house Dickens would probably have made a symbol out of – 'Like Satis House,' she would say, 'except less Christmas cheer.' Magnus liked to say it was more like a pirate ship marooned on land, brim-full with dusty treasures pillaged from past decades, past careers, past lives. 'It's sad,' he would say, 'except it isn't.' And Roxanne would tell him she hoped his audience patter was more insightful than that. Leo, for his part, seldom said anything, but spread his tarot cards before him in that unpleasantly protracted way he sometimes had, and asked whether or not they thought the house wasn't very quietly falling down.

* * *

'A good magician abides by two rules,' Harold said, one pivotal day whose date was never recorded and whose weather beat against windows and made no seasonal sense. 'The first is always the first one and the second is always the second one, and they must absolutely always be remembered in that order, or there's no point remembering them at all.'

He rested back against the edge of his desk and looked at the three of them. They stared straight back at him; Magnus on the edge of his seat, Roxanne peeling at bleedy fingernails, Leo's sheer concentration pulling his mouth down comically at both sides.

'The first rule is this,' Harold said, leaning further back against his desk and knotting his hands together for emphasis, the great protruding veins twisting his fingers sideways and inwards like tree roots when they get too big and start to claw their way up out of the earth. 'Always, always, always have an ending prepared.'

They blinked at him; blue eyes, grey eyes and (in this light) black; and Magnus leant forwards with his elbows on his knees.

'An ending?'

'To the trick, to the act,' Harold said, and the buttons on his waistcoat shone like excited eyes. 'Whatever it might be – cards, sword-swallowing, encasing yourself in cement – everything you do must always be set up with the end clearly in sight. Setting up a magic trick is like winding up a clock. You set the pins and the weights and the levers in place, and you balance everything just so and then when you're absolutely sure that everything is ready, you flick a switch and set it going. And once it's going, there's no way back.'

The clock on the wall above the fireplace seemed suddenly and impulsively to come to life, or possibly just become audible, ticking its rusty way towards half past. Three pairs of eyes slid up towards it before falling again, two by two.

'Magic tricks are funny things,' Harold continued, butterflying fingers across his chest, 'Sometimes, once you wind them up, there's simply no stopping them. That's why it's always better to have a very clear ending prepared so the trick doesn't have to end itself for you. After all, are any of you really so arrogant as to think that if you set a magic trick in motion, it isn't going to find some way to end, with or without your help? That once you set something like that going, it is simply going to stop when you do? How much control do you really think you have?'

'And what's the second rule?' Leo asked, looking left and right at the others as though surprised he had to say it.

Harold smiled.

'The second rule isn't really my business. The second rule is to always have one rule that applies only to you. The second rule you have to come up with on your own. That way, my dears, you'll know what kind of magicians you are. Provided, of course, that you always remember the second rule is no earthly good whatsoever if you don't remember that the first rule has to come first.'

The clock ticked on over the fireplace; skipped a second, two seconds, ticked on again.

* * *

The three of them learned together, in that strange magpie way people will learn when everything is presented to them as if by accident. They came to the house day after day expecting card tricks or mentalism or rabbits in hats and were presented instead with sleight of hand, hypnosis; whatever wasn't on the menu the day before.

'Always have an ending,' Harold would intone again and again, as Roxanne and Magnus roleplayed as two punters with dark secrets and Leo tried to hypnotise them both with a watch on a long strip of felt. 'Know how the trick ends and how you're going to get there. No magician ever did well by leaving things to chance. That's how you end up locked in a concrete box with no way out and an audience getting bored outside. And they're not going to save the escapologist from the box he can't get out of if he's already bored them to tears.'

This last was aimed mainly at Magnus, but he had unfortunately fallen into a daze thanks to Leo's still-swinging stopwatch.

'So tell me, kind sir, have you ever killed anyone?' Leo asked, in that strange stage voice he had cultivated which sounded always as though he had just burned the roof of his mouth.

'No,' Magnus replied.

'I could set him up right now so he'd murder anyone I wanted if he heard a trigger word,' Leo said, waving a hand before Magnus' frozen features with ill-concealed glee. 'I *won't*,' he added, catching Roxanne's eye and pulling a face that was all teeth and quite unsavoury. 'But I could.'

He snapped his fingers and Magnus came back.

* * *

Roxanne liked to disappear. The psychology of the thing was simple, really – lanky girl, too-tall-at-school girl, nowhere-to-hide girl – but the question of making the act itself look like more than just one big Freudian slip through the floorboards was frankly of greater concern.

Harold had found her working as a glamorous assistant to a second-rate, end-of-the-pier type chancer who sawed her in half for lunchtime audiences, paid her pocket money and felt her up with his gloves still on. White-blonde and bony-wristed, she had looked terrible in spangles and miserable every minute she was on stage – apart from the moment when she was shut inside a box and made to magically disappear.

That sudden empty box – an overwhelming absence of spangled sullenness behind its hinging door – had looked better on her than a smile. After the show, Harold had accosted her coming out of the stage door (knock-knees and blunt pelvis wrapped up in black velour) and asked her if she'd ever thought more seriously about disappearing. She had looked at him frankly and told him she didn't think seriously about very much else.

So now, with Harold's help, she worked on it, collecting tools like clues to her own kidnapping; flash paper, magic dust, floor mirrors; working always to the specification which, in time, became her Second Rule: *Never be gone for so long that you don't make it back for the curtain call.*

The act that developed out of all this was acrobatic; a girl folding herself in and out of thin air in sudden puffs of steam and smokeless flame, reappearing in and around her audience, throwing her voice and frightening children, over here, up there, right behind you. She took it out to markets and street corners, drew a crowd in Covent Garden as she disappeared outside the Actors' Church and reappeared on the balcony of the market restaurant. The ending was always the same, twisting herself up in a cape that covered her from head to toe, then fell flat on the ground with nothing beneath it, and every time she would reappear in the middle of the audience, leading her own applause with her hair full of blue touch paper.

'One day I'll have a trapdoor to disappear through,' she would say. 'And that'll be my ending. You say Rule One: have an ending, so that'll be mine. No more of this fucking running around.'

'Language,' Harold would intone from the depths of an

armchair, and Roxanne would go on swearing just the same.

* * *

Magnus' ending was a simpler matter, if only because, as an escapologist, if you don't end your act correctly, you usually end up dead.

'I suppose that's what he means by all this *magic's like clockwork, unstoppable, inevitability* stuff – at least where I'm concerned,' he would say as Roxanne shackled him up in Harold's basement and hung him upside down from the rafters like a lamp. 'I mean, if I was stupid enough not to have an ending prepared and an escape route thought out when I chained myself up in a fish tank full of piranhas, then obviously the trick's going to end all by itself whether I like it or not.'

'I don't think that's really what he meant,' Leo would reply, absently chalking out voodoo circles on the floor beneath Magnus' head. But, by then, Magnus would be far too intent on freeing himself to listen and Leo never really meant him to hear anyway.

Harold had found Magnus working in Camden as a shill for a man who would swallow anything his audience gave him; a trick Roxanne later said sounded less akin to magic than a free lunch. Magnus (tall, orphaned, magisterial) had been charged with the task of dressing down and loitering about at the back of crowds to offer up watches, penknives and other trick items designed to compress or dissolve in the mouth. The audience, on a good day, would be so filled with schadenfreude at the idea of some moron letting a street magician swallow his Rolex that they would usually pay up out of amusement alone. Of course, on bad days, other people would demand the magician swallow *their* watches or take it upon themselves to demand Magnus's watch back for him and then, usually, there was a fight. It had been at these times, as the crowd around the magician crushed inwards, that Harold had first begun to notice that Magnus, always at the very heart of the throng just seconds before, would suddenly be standing somewhere all the way across the street, usually with a cigarette going and his watch safe on his wrist.

It had been during a particularly rowdy showdown in which someone from the crowd seemed to have decided that the Heimlich manoeuvre was the only sure-fire way of wresting the magician's ill-gotten gains from him that Harold had finally made contact. Magnus had been leaning up against a lamppost staring at his shoes and had looked up with an expression quite devoid of interest when Harold cleared his throat.

'Not a prostitute,' Magnus had said, in a voice that was more apologetic than irritated. 'I know I'm standing underneath a lamppost and it's Camden and I'm pretty and everything, but I'm not. Sorry. Try down the road.'

'Ah – no,' Harold had said. 'No, that's not what I was… looking for.'

'Oh, sorry. What then?'

'Well, you know, I was watching you in that crowd just now, I was watching you *escape* that crowd just now, and I was just wondering whether you'd ever thought about escapology?'

He had, of course, and hanging upside down in Harold's basement soon became his daily exercise, tangled up in Chubb locks and medieval manacles that Harold had previously been using as coffee-table talking points.

'I think my Second Rule should probably just be "Don't die",' Magnus once said, clambering down from the basement rafters with one arm still chained to an ankle. 'But that's stupid so I'll say it like this: "Rule One; always have an ending. Rule Two; make sure that ending isn't death." I think it's quite poetic.'

With a little wriggle, he freed his arm, straightening up with much manful rubbing of wrists and stepping right into the centre of Leo's voodoo chalk circle, smudging a gap straight through the line.

* * *

Sometimes, they liked to drink together and try to catch each other out.

Harold, you must remember, was a little shy of ninety and on the none-too-infrequent evenings when an armchair lecture became an armchair nap, Roxanne, Leo and Magnus had few real scruples about wandering into his kitchen and having a go at the cooking brandy. They would sit around the table in the disused parlour, surrounded on all sides by old show banners, magic wands in glass cases, severed limbs made of rubber and sellotape, and try to see through each other's card tricks, drinking from glass tumblers and talking louder than they needed to be heard.

'You've never told us your second rule,' Magnus would slur, as Leo upturned three dusty eggcups from the sideboard and asked him to pick which had the dead fly underneath. 'I've got one and

Roxy's got one, but you never tell.'

'Nope, sorry,' Leo would smirk as Magnus tapped the second eggcup, lifting it up to reveal nothing beneath.

'You don't, though,' Roxanne would concur. 'You don't even have a speciality. I mean, I'm an illusionist and Magnus is an escapologist and you just sort of sit there with your tarot cards or your chalk or your voodoo. Smirking. You're always doing something, Leo, but I don't see what it is. What are you working on, Leo? What are you trying to be?'

Leo would smirk again as Magnus tapped the first and third eggcups, lifting them both simultaneously to reveal nothing, before opening his mouth to show the fat, black fly quite dead on the tip of his tongue.

* * *

It was already too late to refuse Harold anything, the night he suggested a show. They dragged chairs and lamps and a long, grey ottoman down to the basement and took note of a thousand careful tips on showmanship, all made by Harold from a pose of shrunken command in a great winged armchair with cobwebs dangling gently over his ears.

'Remember always to keep their eyes moving and their ears locked solely on you. Remember not to smile too much – try not to be a smiling magician. A smile is a skull trying to get out onto the face. It reminds your audience there is something beneath your surface and makes them less likely to trust you. And they want to be fooled, remember. It's your job to give them what they want.'

Magnus went first, arranging his chains and pulleys and winching himself up to hang bat-like above his audience with his hands chained behind his neck and ankles, and his eyes fixed always on the floor. He disentangled himself to polite applause, which turned to horrified silence for a split second as he seemed to dangle only from his neck, before letting himself go with a knowing little chuckle and landing flat on his feet to take bows with his hair still upside-down.

Roxanne went next, and a complicated routine followed in which she slid neatly in and out of existence, drawing her audience in one direction, throwing her voice over their shoulders, talking genially about nothing in particular as she dematerialised in a puddle of shadow, reappeared beneath the ottoman, disappeared in a burst of black smog. She finished up sat ramrod-straight in the empty armchair, nodding mutely at her own applause and it wasn't until Leo stood up to take his turn that she allowed herself to relax.

'I'm going to summon the dead,' he said, and his skull shone straight through his face.

There were no tarot cards today, no chalk, no flies, no smirking, just hands together and yawning eyes like the blank front windows of a house for sale.

'What's that?' Harold asked, as though simply hard of hearing. And, as if in deaf solidarity, Leo ignored him.

'I need quiet,' he said, looking from one person to the next. 'And I need each of you to think of someone you've lost who affected you. Someone you loved. Someone you hated, maybe. Someone you need to ask a question. Anyone at all whose death is somehow still a presence. Anyone at all to bring back from the dead.'

'Leo,' Roxanne asked, 'what are you going to—'

Leo snapped his fingers and the room went black.

What happened next would be difficult to say. Total darkness can be tricky like that.

There was a rumbling sensation, thick shadows shuffling through the gloom.

Roxanne made a choked noise. The armchairs creaked beneath them and, somewhere in the centre of the room, Leo made a terrible sound which could have been a groan or a laugh. Something light flashed and vanished, Magnus grunted, the room seemed to swarm with heat and air – darkness rocking like water – there was a clatter, further groaning, a sudden swill of light and smoke and coughing and then, out of nothing, there were three shadowy figures hanging in the air between them.

There was a swell, a silence, a stop – and then Magnus howled '*Mum!*' and Roxanne gasped '*Nana!*' and Harold made a noise that could have been a woman's name and could have been nothing. And then the lights slammed back on and there were no shadowy figures to be seen anywhere, and Leo was laughing so hard he looked like he'd choke.

'What the fuck was that?' Roxanne was already raging, but Leo was, for the minute, laughing too hard even to speak.

'It's so simple,' he gasped, as he finally calmed down, and showed them. Mirrors, a smoke screen, a projector, a little emotional manipulation and pretty much anyone could be made to appear. 'That's what I'm trying to be,' he grinned at Roxanne.

'You asked me, so there it is. I want to be a Necromancer.'

'So what does that make your second rule then, Leo?' Harold's voice came as if from someone partially buried, unreadable eyes fixed on Leo as though he had never quite noticed him before. Leo grinned, ignoring Magnus whose face was now hidden in his hands, ignoring Roxanne who looked like she might never stop wanting to scream.

'Easy,' Leo said, 'Rule Two: Remember that none of it's real.'

'Well that's all very well, my dear,' said Harold with a long, long sigh. 'But for goodness' sake, make sure you always remember Rule One as well.'

* * *

Harold died quite soon after that – unrelated, of course, but all that dust and damp in the basement probably didn't help. He left the three of them almost everything he owned and, once the goods had been divided and the house sold on, everything just sort of broke up.

Magnus, it might interest you to know, went on to find particular success as a TV escapologist, a fact which would surprise exactly no one who had ever seen his huge blue eyes or the gold of his hair when it hung upside down. He drew a solid audience for four series, escaping concrete boxes and live bombs and barbed-wire jackets, until one day, preparing for a standard water-tank escape, he neglected to check with his director what sequence of knots they would be using to rope his wrists to his thighs and, already overrunning by almost an hour on filming, decided he could probably just wing it and figure out the ending on his own. That night, unable to contend with a knot he'd never seen before, he drowned in a water tank of his own design before the studio hands could even fire the intern for tying him up the wrong way.

Roxanne, though not a woman ever destined for TV, did finally get her very own trapdoor, working the circus and burlesque circuits as Roxy Nothing – The Amazing Imaginary Girl in black spangles and a bright-white bun. She did well for several years, folding in and out and back again, moving like the colours in the corner of your eye, until one day, when the team she was with moved into a broken-down Victorian theatre they had chosen largely for effect, she forgot to remind the manager that the ending to her act had changed, assuming instead that even at a theatre like this someone would give him the memo. So it was that one Saturday night, before an excitable audience who would later prove hell to subdue, Roxanne fell through the trapdoor of an unfamiliar stage, landed on bare concrete with no crash mat to stop her and snapped her neck in two. The applause that greeted her apparent final disappearance was long and sustained, but she was unable to reappear in time to receive it.

Leo, meanwhile, carved out an unsettlingly fanatical fanbase as the man who conjured the dead live on stage; an act whose two rules he followed to the letter right up until the day when the mirror broke and the projector stalled and he had no time and he was on stage all of a sudden with a vast audience and no ending and with no idea of what was going to happen next.

'I need quiet,' he said, and his words echoed into nothing. 'And I need each of you to think of someone you've lost who affected you. Someone you loved. Someone you hated, maybe. Someone you need to ask a question. Anyone at all whose death is somehow still a presence. Anyone at all to bring back from the dead.'

The audience's faces were a thousand upturned shadows. He snapped his fingers and the lights went out.

What happened next would be difficult to say (total darkness can be tricky like that).

There was all the usual rumbling. Crashing and muttering and lights on the wall. Several members of the audience gave little shrieks, shushed at once by others; lights flashed and smoke billowed and the ground seemed to shudder underfoot.

And then there they were. Three shadows on the stage before him. Harold, Magnus and Roxanne, smiling at him blandly; three skulls stealing out onto three faces, three endings provided by a trick which would not be left undone.

And, just like that, Leo dropped down dead of fright.

Icebound

Christina Prado

The ice seemed to sigh as he slid on the sugar snow rolling like tiny marbles under his feet. Kasper lay flat out for a second. From this low level, he saw the broken landscape as if caught in a web spun by the sun from the watery channels flowing through the freeze. It seemed to bind the floes together, casting the illusion of unity where there was only division. Lifting himself, fearful of Isak catching up, he carried on running, stumbling over the smaller hummocks and piled-up ice until he saw the polar bear.

Breathing heavily, he raised his rifle to take aim at his true quarry, the old man: arrogant nose and walrus moustache obscured as he bent over the felled beast. This way, Kasper thought, he could claim he'd been gunning for the bear: a terrible accident, the sun on the snow had dazzled him, queered his aim. By God, he would even squeeze out a tear or two if he had to. Then he might stand a chance of making it back home.

He pictured celebrating the New Year with his father, raising a glass to 1898. With this polar expedition under his belt, the coming year would hold untold promise: the bestowal of The Order of the Polar Star, Commander Grand Cross, no less; the Court Medal, maybe; and the highest accolade of them all, the Illis Quorum. Why not? Then invitations to speak on international lecture tours, perhaps the renaming of his old school in Jönköping in his honour. He sighed bitterly. It had all gone to hell.

He had the old man in his sight now. Yet Kasper hesitated. Isak would know the truth. Why the devil had he confided in him?

Last night, alone in the tent with Isak, Kasper had watched him break Cracknel biscuits in half, then add three careful spoonfuls of Mellin's food powder to the water they called soup. Isak looked up ruefully.

'I'm having to cut rations again. Let's hope another bear, or even a seal, crosses our path soon. Until then, I'll have to be even stricter with our portions.'

Kasper answered quickly, mindful the old man might come in at any minute. 'Everything's counted and measured here, Isak. The kilometres we walk, the load we carry, the days behind us. But how many lie ahead? Do you dare count those?'

Isak continued resolutely with his task, as if no words had been spoken. In one stride Kasper was on him, shaking his arm. Some of the biscuits fell onto the groundsheet.

'Wake up man! There are still some weeks of summer left. If we change direction tomorrow, we could make it off the ice to solid ground. Don't you see?'

These words had been knocking against Kasper's teeth for weeks. He had longed to share his doubts since the night they'd dropped onto the ice, yet he'd held off. He was one against two, after all. Isak and the old man had planned the expedition, spent time together with Isak's family in Stockholm: dinners, dances, opera. They were friends, he the newcomer and the youngest. The respect Isak had for his elder was as much a part of him as salt is of the sea. Kasper understood that. This is how they lived at home, where they learnt respect at their fathers' knee. But that was all behind them. Here in the Great White, what did such things matter?

That morning he had woken to find the ice had moved again while they slept, and was moving still. More startling blue fingers were poking their way into the whiteness, running on between the hummocks, making sludge pools and divisions in the floe. The pressure ice groaned and whispered in its movement like a lover answering to the other's caress. Kasper imagined the sea beneath the wrinkled ice sheet becoming restless, shifting and turning in its sleep during the long sunlit hours of polar night. He had taken more meteorological observations and compared them with those meticulously recorded in his expedition notebook, but he already knew the crushing truth: the current was carrying them back across the long distance over which they had stumbled, staggered and crawled. Surely this bitter news would stir Isak into action.

'Isak,' he continued. 'I have to tell you this. There's no easy way to say it. This morning, I discovered… the current, it's taking us back to where we started.'

To his surprise, Isak sat down heavily on the ammunition box as though all the air had been knocked out of him. Not meeting Kasper's eye, he said, 'I know.'

'You know?!'

'I've had weeks to think about it. It's quite logical. We're walking on frozen sea – but not completely so. The water's still alive below, isn't it? And we're floating on it.'

Rubbing a hand over his dry, weathered cheeks, Kasper struggled to contain his anger. 'You knew it and I know it. Then the old man must know too. God in Heaven, Isak! We're not even meant to be here. I signed up for an aerial expedition, not this circus. We were supposed to be over the Pole in three days. Three days! He doesn't even believe in Arctic exploration, does he? You said he was only ever interested in what his precious air balloon could do. We don't even have the right equipment down here, for God's sake.'

Isak sighed.

'Listen carefully and hear me, Isak, because of this you can be certain – when that sun goes down under the horizon, it'll be the end of us. We won't survive the winter out here.'

'He won't change his mind, that's what I'm certain of,' said Isak. 'I know him. He's stubborn.'

'Stop thinking and just act,' Kasper hissed. 'If we take our sledges and set off, he'll have to follow.'

'He won't.'

'He'll follow.'

'He'll die if we leave him.'

'He will follow. Trust me.'

'I won't leave him.' Isak stood up and turned away, busying himself with heating the soup. 'You need to get the spoons out.'

'And Katrine?' Kasper murmured softly. 'Do you really mean to make a widow of her before your first anniversary? Think of her and save yourself. There's no one else here to see what we do. Or don't do.'

'Tell me this, then, Kasper.' Isak faced him, his cracked lips flaking as he spoke. 'Let's suppose we do as you propose. Then what? Do you truly imagine you and I could take our place again amongst family and friends if we commit this murder? Because that's what it will be if we leave him behind. Kill him and you kill everything good about our lives. We'll never be able to go back to what we had – whether anyone else sees or not.' He held up his left hand, the tips of his fingers bandaged where the frost had bitten. 'I'd rather die than dishonour this wedding ring like that. Either way, we're dead. To the world we knew. You may as well face it.'

'You'll feel differently when we're free of him. You'll see,' said Kasper, stepping away.

'Kill him and I'll have to kill you. And it will be your doing.' Isak's voice was high and strained. He laughed at the look of disbelief on Kasper's face. 'Yes. You'll have made yourself a murderer. How could I ever trust you after that? I'd always have to guard against you. Always. Even if we do make it back home. Don't you see? He would follow us alright: in our dreams and every waking second he'd be there, between me and you and every tiny detail of our future lives. Don't make a murderer of me. Don't kill my honour, Kaspar. It's all I have.'

Isak stared fixedly into Kasper's eyes and was about to speak again when the tent flap lifted and the old man came in. Isak bent to pick up the biscuits. Kasper pulled on his gloves and limped outside, feeling the burn of his blistered, bloodied feet.

Since then they'd barely spoken, their paltry supper eaten in silence. Later, while the old man wrote in his journal, Isak cleaned and oiled his rifle, which he kept close by him. He took his time over this, methodically exposing the metal parts, rubbing them over with a soft rag, lubricating them. He paid particular attention to the firing mechanism, from time to time raising the gun, looking down its length and through the sight. Curiously, he went through this ritual mostly by touch and instinct because his eyes seldom left Kasper's face.

Discomforted by this unwavering scrutiny, Kasper retreated early to his sleeping sack. There he became irritated by the scratching sound of the old man's pencil moving over the page. Through the downy layers he could still hear the sound: scribble, scribble. Kasper pictured the old man's words being forced to wander relentlessly across the pale pages. Does he write the truth in that blasted book? What does he choose to say about us? His aren't the only words, he thought. Mine have been scratched on the ice, sunk into the snow. He pulled his sleeping sack over his head, escaping Isak's stare and silently mouthing to himself words of his own, unrecorded, known only to him.

This morning, after a meagre breakfast, the old man volunteered to scout out a safe route through the melting ice, leaving them to break camp and pack the sledges for the day's march.

After a while, Isak paused to wipe the sweat from his forehead. 'Looks like this infernal sunshine will make the ice difficult again. At least we don't have to wear coats.' He dropped his voice. 'Kasper, you may as well know. I've talked it over with him. He won't change course. He's sticking to the plan.'

Kasper felt light, insubstantial. In his mind, he already didn't exist. It was as though his body had turned to liquid and was evaporating under the ever-present sun. He looked around at the wide, deep, blue sky, at the diverse and dazzling shades of white encircling them, and felt the very opposite of freedom. He couldn't take it much longer. He must convince Isak. It was a perfect day not to die.

'There is no plan, Isak. We can't allow this folly to continue. We must make our own plan, you and I. Without further delay. Without the old fool's seal of approval.'

Isak came at him. Kasper had never seen him so angry. He was pleased: at last he had goaded the poor, misguided blockhead into action. He drew back, but Isak grabbed a handful of his jersey, pulling him close, talking low and with menace.

'Happy enough to play the adventurer though, weren't you? I saw the way you preened in front of the public – thousands of them on the harbour side. Did you really think they were there for you? Without him, there'd be no expedition. Just in it for the glory, weren't you?'

Kasper stood his ground, pressing his advantage. He tried again, appealing to Isak's fanciful nature. 'Remember that first night up in the balloon? You told me such tales! That we might find here monstrous beasts. Half-formed men. A secret way to the centre of the Earth. Or perhaps the very site of Paradise, supreme beings beautiful beyond compare. Yes, you said all that! Then you said, "In truth, no man yet knows what lies here at the roof of the world." Well I do. I do know Isak. We've been crawling about on this godforsaken ice for weeks and I'm telling you we won't find giants or dragons or spirits from other worlds. All we'll find here is our own death. For the last time: it's him or us.'

'And I told you before, I won't abandon him.' Isak pulled away.

Kasper picked up his fallen rifle. 'I can solve that dilemma for you.'

'You'd better not.' Isak turned towards him, his face drained of colour. He had his own rifle in his hand. 'Otherwise there'll be consequences.'

They stood glaring at one another, rifles in hand: two young men who might never grow old, immobile under the Arctic sun.

A shot rang out. Kasper felt a bubble of impossible hope rising within him. He saw the same emotion flash across Isak's face. They waited, listening intently; desperate for the terminal silence that would release them both. Another shot sounded.

They both started running heavily in the direction taken by their elder. Without warning, Kasper threw all his weight into Isak, knocking him to the ground, leaving him behind. He had to get there first.

Now here he stood, taking careful aim. He felt wraithlike, invisible. His head filled with that first night in the balloon, how they had soared higher and further above the sparkling earth than any man before them. A record-breaking flight. From the safety of the wicker gondola they declared they could face death with equanimity, having achieved so much. How strange it had been to look down on the sea as it lost itself in the freeze. The night air had been cold and crisp like the apple before the bite. The guidelines rattled in the snow, the wind whined through the weave of the basket. He'd wondered shyly whether the others could hear the beat of his proud, triumphant heart.

Today, all at once, he understood what they had found here at the top of the globe. It was the life force of the natural world: elemental, terrifying, hostile to human endeavour. In a high, thin voice only he could perceive, it was screaming at him, mocking him. His bones answered white to white.

He saw through his sight the old man raise his head and wave. 'The beast still breathes! Come and help.'

Behind him, Kasper heard the sound of a firing pin being cocked. Isak had arrived. Slowly, he lowered his own gun, but kept a firm grip on it. Side by side, they walked towards the old man and his prize. He turned to them, rheumy eyes wide, the tips of his brown moustache frosted as though they had been dipped in sugar.

'*En garde!*' he said. 'This brute is not yet done for.' He gestured impatiently. 'Come on! Why are you waiting?'

Kasper watched as the animal raised its head and tried to put weight on its front paws. It was a magnificent bear, their best so far. It would give them meat for many days. More fuel to prolong their futile endeavours. The sight of its senseless suffering drew the surrounding icy coldness deep into his very being.

Swiftly, he stepped back behind his companions, raised his rifle and dispatched the two bullets in rapid succession. The discharge echoed across the landscape, distant ice floes answering with the thunderous rumbling fury of faraway gods. He thrust his rifle nose down into the snow where it remained, tilted like a broken cross.

As he stood over the dying animal, Kasper saw himself reflected in the last light of its eyes: a tiny little man and all around him the impenetrable white wastes stretching to infinity. Then the bear's eyes clouded, the light faded and he was gone.

Inspired by the 1897 Andrée expedition, this story is entirely a work of fiction and no resemblance to any person, living or dead, is intended.

Pearl

Stephen Jones

I had a girlfriend once. No, that's a lie. It was twice. The first one looked at me one day and said: 'You just miss it. Do you know that? You're almost good-looking, but you miss it.' So with the second one I thought, I know how it's done now. 'Can I tell you something,' I said to her when I'd run out of other things to say. 'You're not pretty. You almost are, but you just miss it.'

That was before I started the watching.

It was my last night with the Roberts. That wasn't their real name, but it was a name that came at me through the glass one night. So someone must have shouted it: Robert! And after that they were the Roberts to me. Their real name was Berlin. That's the same as the capital of Germany. You can find out anyone's real name if you know where to look. Most people don't take their name and address off the letters they put into their recycling. It might be junk mail, but that doesn't matter. It's still your name. Your identity. I always tear it off mine. It makes a little jagged hole at the top of the page. And from the envelope. Though that's more in the middle. Then I tear up the name and address and drop the pieces into two different bins.

That's one thing about the watching. The lack of sound. Generally you can only get the odd word. Or if someone shouts. Which they do, quite a lot on some screens. But most of the time it's like the old days of silent films. Except it's not in black and white. And they move differently. They move normally, not in little jerky movements like they do in those films.

I'd been with the Roberts for nearly two weeks; but there was something about them that I didn't like. They didn't watch television like they do on most screens. They didn't even have it on in the background. And they all ate at once, the whole family, sitting down together and eating dinner at 6.30 every night. Just like they used to back in the day. I looked it up; researched it. The father would sit at the head of the table and the mother at the other end. The Roberts had a round table though, so that wasn't possible.

It wasn't because they didn't watch television that I didn't like the Roberts. It was them I didn't like: Mum, Dad, the one called Robert and the other two children, one boy and one girl. Sitting down and eating and talking. 'Pass the potatoes will you Robert?' 'Yes, certainly Mummy, right away.' A family – together. And me outside, on my knees, looking in. It made me feel that I was only half a person. Less than that.

So it was time to move on. There were only two or three weeks left before the season was going to end. The watching only really works during the dark months either side of Christmas. It's when it gets dark early that people have their lights on and the curtains open. Later on in the evening most of them close their curtains. Perhaps it makes them feel safer. Or maybe they're worried that someone might be peering in at them. Also, the later it is the quieter it gets, the fewer people there are around. So there's more chance of someone noticing you, or hearing some sound you might accidentally make. Avoiding risk, that's the secret of successful watching. That was how I'd managed to watch 49 screens over four seasons without a problem. Them inside, me outside. And none of them having any idea I was there. And all of them properly documented. Times, dates, people; what they did, what they ate, what they wore. What they said, when I could catch it. Everything I could remember once I got home. All entered up in the database. I called the file 'TV Times'. That was a joke.

Time to move on then. I'd done my research. There's plenty of time during the close season to select the prospects. That was all in the database too. In a separate file. If you're going to do the research properly, you have to do a lot of walking. Street after street. Watching, looking at the buildings, their entrances and exits. Seeing who goes in and comes out. Working out the angles, the watching points, the emergency exits. Then, as soon as the clocks go back and the pomegranates start to gather dust in the greengrocers, you watch the trailers. I like that. Sometimes I think I like the trailers even more than the main feature. No adverts. No popcorn. Just life in the raw. Those programmes on TV – the ones they call 'reality' – they're not real at all. They're a con. A set-up. I know: I've researched it. They choose the people, the locations, the situations they put them in. Then it's all edited down and packaged up and put in front of the punters as reality. But it's what I see that's real. Real life. As it happens. Right there in front of me. Yes it can be boring sometimes. But that's where the trailers come in. Where a selection can be made. But it's me who makes it. Me, not them.

Pearl's screen wasn't boring. When I watched her trailer they were having a row. Her and her mother. That's how I knew her name right away. 'Pearl,' her mother was shouting, 'you're too young to be wearing that stuff.' They were both close up to the window so I could hear everything they said. Her mum had a little bottle in one hand and a piece of cotton wool in the other. Pearl was looking across at her with a pout on her lips. She held up a hand, in front of her. She had long slim fingers, and the tips, the nails, were painted a bright-red colour. They looked like the throat of an exotic bird. 'They look good on me,' Pearl said. 'All my friends say so.'

'Pearl.' Her mother had stopped shouting, but she was still talking in a loud voice. 'You're ten years old.'

Pearl looked at her. The look was like acid in your face, a blade between your ribs. 'That's the whole point,' she said.

So that was it. I ditched the Roberts right away. I was feeling a bit panicky though with so little of the season left. I'd found Pearl, but in two weeks, three at the most, I would have to lose her again.

It was the first night of the main feature. Outside the house I looked carefully both ways. The street was deserted. A scrap of paper blew past on the wind and I put my foot down hard to trap it. I went in through the gate, closing it silently behind me. It had a metal latch that would click if you just let it go. At the side there were two doors. One was at the top of a set of concrete steps. The other was at ground level. That one was Pearl's. They're called maisonettes. It's a French word. I looked it up. It means 'little house'. But they're not little houses at all, more like two flats. As I rounded the back wall I could see immediately that the curtains hadn't been drawn. It was February 27th. In a few more weeks it would be light at this time.

I crouched down at the bottom corner nearest to the way I'd have to run if it came to it. That's the best place for watching. They were sitting apart, heads down, not talking. Pearl's mum was reading a book. Pearl had a pen in her hand, though she wasn't doing much writing. She put the end in her mouth, took it out, put it down, picked it up again so that she was holding it when her mother turned towards her and said something I couldn't hear. Pearl shrugged, then turned her face directly towards the window. Her skin was a light-brown colour, different to her mother's, which was just white. She had a lot of black hair, which stood out from her head. Her eyes – it was the first time I had really seen her eyes – were brown. They were looking but not looking at the same time.

Pearl's mum put down her book and said something else. Her voice was louder than before, and I just caught the word 'homework'. Then she went out of the room, closing the door behind her. For a moment Pearl just sat there, listening. When her Mum didn't reappear, she pushed her book away and took out her phone from a bag down by her chair. She put some music on that I'd never heard before. I didn't like it, but that didn't matter. It was Pearl's choice. Pearl's music. She looked towards the door again, then started to move in time to the music. She was only ten, but she danced like a grown-up, moving her head, her arms, her whole body. It was like a picture and a poem at the same time. The dance only lasted a minute or so. Pearl must have heard something then, because she turned the music off, put the phone back in her bag and sat down at the table. As she did so the door opened and her mum came back in carrying an ironing board and an iron. Pearl had picked up her pen, eyes on the book in front of her. Her mother said something, put down the ironing things and came straight up to the window. I knew what was going to happen then, but still it was a shock. First she pulled the curtain nearest to me, then the other one. So that was it: show over. You always feel cheated when that happens, because someone else has decided when it ends, not you. And you know that the action is still going on, only you're not allowed to see it any more.

Normally I go straight home at the end of a show and enter the details on the computer. But that night I just walked around the streets for a long time. At one point I went into the park, the little one they never lock at night because there aren't any gates. It was dark in there and I sat on a bench and looked up at the stars. There were so many of them, so many and so far away. I like stars. Stars are so much easier than people. I started counting. When I got to one thousand, four hundred and thirty seven I gave up and walked home.

How many sessions did I have left with Pearl? The next night was horrible, one of the worst of my life. There were people outside her gate when I arrived: three stupid old women in coats and scarves, just standing there talking. I walked round the block, but they were still there when I got back. Didn't they have any homes to go to? I stayed away for longer the second time, forcing myself to walk past three turnings before coming back around again. They were still there, blocking the pavement. I could feel the panic start to rise inside me. In the past I'd have just given up and gone home, but now I felt like shouting at them, kicking their fat ankles. When I had almost reached them again, they split apart and went their separate ways. One went into the house next to Pearl's. The other two walked slowly off together. I followed them for a while, keeping my distance, only turning back when they were completely clear of the area.

I knew something was wrong as soon as I rounded the building. There was no oblong of yellow spilling out onto the lawn, just a horrible dark patch where there should have been light. Up close I could see that the curtains weren't drawn, but there was no light on in the room. They must be out. But where could they be? What was her mother thinking of? It was a Wednesday, and she'd have school the next day. I waited for almost an hour, but there was no sign of them returning. Then it started to rain, an oily, cold drizzle that slid straight down my neck and onto my shoulders. I trudged home, a slick of damp clinging to my back.

But Thursday was different. So different it almost made up for woeful Wednesday. When I arrived they were having another row, a full-blown shouting match, loud enough for me to hear everything that was said. On Wednesday they'd been at Pearl's school for parents' evening. The problem was maths. Pearl wasn't working hard enough. Or so her mother said. How could she expect to get into the grammar school when her maths was so poor? Pearl said she didn't care. About the maths, or the grammar school. Most of her friends were going to the comprehensive anyway. Her mum really started shouting then. What did she expect to do with her life if she only wanted to follow her friends? Pearl went quiet for a moment, then said something beautiful. 'I don't want to do,' she said, looking straight at her mother. 'I just want to be.'

As I walked home my head hummed with possibilities. Pearl

was not good at maths. At least not as good as she should be. But I was. At school, maths was the only thing I was good at. So maybe I could teach Pearl how to be better. This idea was so stunning, so perfect, so brimful of possibilities that I had to pause for a moment and cling on to a lamppost just to stop myself from falling over. By the time I was back in my room I had worked it all out. Each time I'd seen her, Pearl was wearing the purple uniform of the local primary school: St Hilda's Church of England it said on the board outside. What they were short of in primary schools were men. I'd read about it. They were also short of people who specialised in maths. That was in the same article. I sat and wrote an email. I was hoping to go to college in the autumn to train as a teacher. I was a maths graduate but hadn't yet had any experience of working with young children. If they could give me a placement for a few weeks I could work with small groups to help improve their maths. I thought I'd be particularly good with the children who'd be going up to secondary school in September. Such an arrangement (I was proud of that phrase) could be mutually beneficial to both the children and me. I read it through again, then added 'or individuals' after the word 'groups'. I found the school's email address on their website and pressed send.

Two days later they got back to me. If I called the school secretary she'd arrange for me to come in for an interview with the head. The room they put me in smelt of dirt and disinfectant. The woman who saw me wasn't the head teacher, but her deputy. Her hands were fat, her fingers short and stubby, and she had a little pink knobbly thing in the middle of her chin. Where had I studied for my degree? she wanted to know. 'London,' I replied. 'Which college?' she asked. 'The best one,' I said. 'Did I have a CRB?' 'Yes,' I said. 'Did I know what a CRB was?' Yes, of course I did. She said she'd be in touch with me the next day. She wasn't.

So then I knew I had to do something else. Only I didn't know what. I went back the next night and the one after that. On the second night Pearl was left alone for a long time. She walked around the room and talked on her phone. Then she put on her music and danced for me again. That made me feel very peculiar. Nothing like this had ever happened to me before. With the watching in the past I had always been in control of it. Now it was controlling me.

I'd never have thought about going inside though if it hadn't been for the keys. On the next night Pearl was holding them, jangling them, annoying her mother. They'd already had words about something I couldn't quite make out. 'Don't do that,' her mother suddenly shouted. 'Just go and put them back where they belong. You know where I mean. On the hook in the hall.'

Up in my room I entered the details: '... put them back... on the hook in the hall.' There were only eight days left now. Ten if I really stretched it. I remembered a pamphlet that had come through the door a few days earlier. From our local police team it had said, giving advice on home security. There was a lot of stuff about fixing locks on doors and windows, then something about not hanging keys up in hallways. Apparently people had been coming round with fishing rods, feeding them in through the letter box, unhooking the door keys and using them to let themselves in. It had been meant as a warning, but to me it looked more like a set of instructions.

In the fishing tackle shop he wanted to sell me everything: rod, line, reel – even something that wriggled to hang on my hook. 'Just the rod,' I said. He gave me a look, then took me to the rack where the rods were displayed. 'That's it,' I said picking out one that looked sufficiently long and springy. 'I haven't told you about the different properties of them yet,' he said. 'Don't bother wrapping it,' I said.

It was in three sections, which made it easier to carry around without being noticed. There was a bag for that, made of canvas, which I also bought. I practised downstairs in the communal hallway when no one else was around, lifting keys off a hook three or four paces away from me. At first the keys kept falling off and clattering to the ground, but after a while I worked out how to keep them on the end of the rod while I pulled it back in towards me. I sat on the hall floor, in the dark, and thought the whole thing through. I had to do it as soon as it got dark, because I needed to get to the key cutter's before he closed. The little kiosk was run by an Asian, so he stayed open later than most of the other shops in the precinct. The real problem though was to do with returning the original set after the new ones had been cut. I couldn't keep them because once Pearl's mother realised they were missing she'd change the locks – bound to. There was only one thing for it: I'd have to go inside the hallway myself and put them back on the hook. I looked up at the pale oblong of glass in the front door and thought about what that would mean. Going inside. Inside the house where Pearl lived.

There was no one on the street this time. I checked the back of the house first. The lights were on, the curtains open and they were both sitting in their usual places. I moved back round to the door. A pool of dark had settled on this side of the house. This helped, but if someone passing looked hard enough, they could still spot me feeding the rod in through the letterbox. The hallway was unlit, but I had thought about that and brought along a little pen torch that I taped on to the end section of the rod.

My light picked out the keys straight away, but the hook was halfway along the passage, which meant that I had to get my hand right in through the letterbox to manoeuvre the tip close enough to make contact. The rod bounced gently up and down under the weight of the torch. After a moment it steadied and I could lever it up to the right height, make contact with the keys and lift them clear. But almost immediately the rod began to shake again. They were heavier than the bunch I had practised with, causing the tip to bend sharply under the weight. If they fell off, I would have no chance of lifting them up again from the floor. I tried to hold the rod as steady as I could, but the thin bit at the end just kept wobbling up and down. A raised voice – Pearl's – sounded from another room, followed by the slamming of a door. Was she about to burst into the hallway, flooding it with light? I heard another door slam, then nothing. Bit by bit, as quickly as I dared, I pulled the rod back out through the letterbox.

I walked calmly back out through the gate and round the corner. Then I ran as fast as I could towards the precinct, throwing the rod into a garden on the way. 'You are lucky to catch me so late young man,' the key cutter said. He charged me £10.35 for the three keys on the ring. Back at the door I put my ear against the cold, hard surface. Nothing. I went round the back, but the curtains had been drawn. I listened one more time, then slid the Yale key into the lock. The door opened easily, noiselessly. I went in, slipped the original keys back onto the hook and let myself out. I had been inside for no more than six seconds.

All the way home I had my hand in my pocket, pressing the hardness of the keys against my palm. I had been inside Pearl's home. Stood where she had stood. And now I could go back in there any time I liked.

For the moment, though, there was no need. There were still six days of the watching season left. On two of the nights the curtains were drawn. On the other four I feasted my eyes, staying for a glorious three hours one evening, all the way through to Pearl's bedtime. I didn't stop on the day I should have stopped, but went back for two more nights even though it wasn't properly dark. I knew it was stupid, against all the rules; but still I went.

Then it was over. I sat in my room and looked at the keys. I told myself that I wasn't going to use them. I'd had my bit of fun. And what could I expect to get out of going inside? I was a watcher, not a burglar.

I lasted for thirteen-and-a-half days. Then I started walking up and down outside St Hilda's at the end of the school day. Once I saw her, with a gang of other girls, and my heart leapt. But someone might notice if I did that too often. And what was to stop that bitch who'd done the interview coming out and spotting me on the other side of the road? Another week went by, sitting in my room looking at the keys. On the eighth day I picked them up, examined them and put them in my pocket. It was midday. That was a good time. The house would be empty till well after four. As

I approached the maisonettes, the woman next door came out. She looked at me, harder than she needed to, and for a moment I thought she was going to say something, but no, she just looked, then went on her way up the street. I walked round the block and when I got back she was gone.

I went in through the gate, up to the door and let myself in. From the hall I went straight through into the living room and sat down at the table. I looked across at the window, letting my eyes wander down to the bottom right-hand corner. It felt so strange to be on the other side of the glass, looking out, not in. I stayed there for over an hour. I had arrived in the house at 12.47 and when I looked at my watch again it was almost 2.00. Out in the hall I pushed at one door, saw it was the kitchen, then investigated the bathroom next door. In Pearl's mum's room there was a bed, a wardrobe and a dressing table with little bottles and tubs neatly arranged. I knew I shouldn't go into the only other room – knew I couldn't stop myself. The curtains were half-drawn. The bed hadn't been made and there were clothes everywhere. She had her own little table and chair. I turned the chair around so that it faced away from the table. Then I sat and let the feeling of being there, in Pearl's room, in Pearl's chair, wash over me. This was different. In all the years of watching, of feeding on other people's lives, there had never been anything like this.

I gazed around the room. It was wonderful being there, but still I could feel there was something that wasn't quite right. I knew what it was. It was the mess. How could she live like this, with all her things strewn about the place? I was only going to do it with one item. No one would notice, no one would remember if it was only one. I picked up a crumpled school blouse from the floor and laid it carefully on the bed. Using small, stroking movements I smoothed it flat, folded in the arms, then another fold across the middle. When I turned it over the collar sat neatly in the centre. I found a half-open drawer with other clothes and put it on the top. I was almost at the door when I noticed the toy elephant. It was sticking out from under the wardrobe and it looked so… wrong just lying there. Would Pearl really remember where she had left it amongst all this clutter? I picked it up, felt the smooth pink felt beneath my fingers, set it upright on the table.

I was going to leave it for at least a week before I went back. But I couldn't wait that long. The two days I did let pass were endless, just empty space, hour after tedious hour. Everything looked the same as I approached. There were two cars and a van parked outside. No one was in either of the cars, but I couldn't see into the van. As I turned the key and let the door swing open I heard footsteps on the path behind me. Then a hand, a large hand with dark hair on the backs of the fingers, clamped itself over mine: 'We'd like a word with you young man.'

The Cherry Stone

Kate Hamer

Morning. Nadine leaves her bright, sunlit apartment on the fifth floor.

Her heels tap on the stone steps that wind down the spine of the building. Past the fourth-floor apartment: the one that is permanently shut and empty, and smells of gas. Where a fly buzzes around the joint of the door. Madame G is standing outside the front door of her own third-floor apartment. She is unflinching in a blue apron, her feet in sturdy black lace-ups planted in the soapy suds on the doorstep. She gives a surly nod, making Nadine feel ridiculous in her own close-fitting yellow dress and high heels, with her basket for market tucked over her arm.

The tiny stone virgin, crusted with age, watches her leave from its niche by the main door.

Out on the street the feeling is still with her. The sun strikes at the ground bright and hot as she walks towards the market. It's where she'll buy dinner for her and Marc. A small cut of meat, lean and well-chosen. Salad. A tart with caramelised glistening peaches.

Awful woman, Nadine is not speaking out loud, but feels as if any moment she might. *Why can't she leave me alone? Always standing there.* Her heels ring on the pavement and her black hair bounces on her back.

The dark shadow of a statue slips over her as she passes. A city elder of Marseilles: the heavy stones of his eyes contemplating what has become of the place where he was born.

When a face floats up from the ground she just misses treading on it. One more step and her shoe would have planted right in the middle, spearing the flesh with her heel. She stands still with shock, one foot raised.

'Gabriel!'

He's in a hole in the ground she hadn't even seen – like the ones brewers roll their barrels down. He gazes up with the wrinkle-eyed paleness of a cellar creature not used to the white blaze of sun on his face. There must be steps down there because he walks upwards until his chest is the same height as the street.

'Nadine?' He blinks up. 'Is it you? I haven't seen you since... was it school?'

He opens up his arms. A laugh rises up from Nadine's throat – it's strange to see just his torso growing up out of the ground. He smiles, and thin lines net his eyes. 'Why don't you come down? It's so hot out here.'

She hesitates, still flustered. 'Okay. For a minute.'

With one easy movement he vaults off the stairs. His hands, fixing onto the lip of the hole, take his weight for a second. Then he drops down below. He seems strong and wiry. Tentative at first, scared of falling, she places her foot on the first step of the stone staircase disappearing down into black. A white hand comes out of the dark and she holds on lightly with two fingers, for balance.

At first, below, her eyes are blinded from the sunlight. Gradually the outline of a large wooden table emerges. Then the blades of Gabriel's cheekbones float into view, pale under heavy dark hair. Something glows red in the middle of the table: a pewter plate piled with cherries.

'Please sit...' He lights a cigarette, another red point in the dark. Almost immediately the smoke is sucked towards the hole and up to the street.

He sits opposite her on one of the wooden chairs grouped round the table, as if in readiness for a supper party. Now she can see Gabriel properly, he looks old for his age.

'School seems such a time ago. When did we leave?' she asks, touching her own face lightly.

'Perhaps nine, ten years?' He sucks at his cigarette. 'So did you go to university? Was it history you used to talk about?'

She shakes her head. 'I never went – most of the others have left, I think. I imagined I was the only one left. But you stayed too?'

He grins. 'I'm a bar monkey. I wash glasses and pour wine for tourists. I don't mind; it suits me.'

'I'm married now.'

'What about kids?' he asks.

'No. Nothing.'

'It's good to see you again. It reminds me, well...' He smiles and his skin folds like origami. '...you forget it's possible you were ever really young.' He pushes the plate across the table towards her. 'Take one, they're refreshing.'

The skin of the cherry feels cold against her teeth as she bites into it. The jelly of the flesh is cold too, delicious. It's so cool in here, away from the bright sunlight close by. The walls of the cellar are coated with dampness so they look like they're sweating. For the first time she notices a faded green door behind Gabriel, made of metal.

'What's through that door?'

'Oh, that goes to my place.'

There's a silence and she sees him withdrawing back inside himself, after the temporary diversion of her appearance. It's happened quickly. 'Marseilles stinks this time of year,' he says.

She sticks her nose into the air and sniffs. But all she gets is a dusty odour of mildew.

Monday: dove-grey fitted dress with white collar. Tuesday: green striped blouse and white skirt, beige high heels. Wednesday: jeans, faux peasant blouse. Thursday: camel silk dress…

Every day takes her back to the cellar. She stands looking in, like a woman about to drown herself in a lake but this seems the only place in the whole city where she wants to be. Then, the ripe cherries; Gabriel making his cigarette glow bright at the end.

They have been silent for a while when Gabriel asks, 'Do you remember the Cloutier woman at elementary?'

Nadine liked the silence, it had not been strained, but when he asks about their teacher she sits up. 'Yes, yes, I haven't thought about her in years.'

There's a memory of light streaming through a high-up window illuminating the wisps of hair falling around Madame Cloutier's head. The teacher's hand is reaching up, almost in a wave. She has been standing like that, immobile, for almost ten minutes. The children are starting to whisper and laugh out loud.

'She just disappeared. What happened to her?' says Nadine.

One day a man was standing in her place and he was saying,

'*Bonjour la classe*. I am Monsieur Albert. I am to be your new teacher.' His feet were neat and placed closely together. His face didn't invite questioning. He opened a book and continued with the grammar lesson they'd been working on the day before and it was as if Madame Cloutier had never existed.

Gabriel shrugs. 'She probably went to the madhouse. I hope she's still there. She didn't like me at all.'

'Why not? You were just a little boy!'

'Why not? She hated Jews, of course. It didn't matter how old I was.'

'But…'

'But nothing. It never goes away. It's like gas under our feet. It's here, now, in Marseilles – just waiting to be released.'

She knows what he means. Marseilles is full of secrets. They sleep down dark alleys, they bubble up from the cracks in pavements. She has her own. Lately she feels people have begun to see through her like an X-ray to the curled ghost inside of her, the thing that was picked out like a pomegranate seed on a pin. Soon, Marc will catch a glimpse of it too. The thought sets her heart racing.

They sit in silence for a minute and the sounds from outside permeate; cars tooting, footsteps, little chunks of conversation. Slowly, her heart returns to a normal speed. Nadine feels they have come close to having an argument. Gabriel didn't raise his voice but the cigarette in his hand jerked from the way his fingers snapped together. She wants for this all to blow past them so she doesn't have to leave.

'How often do you go out?' she asks, biting into cherry. The sweet sour juice is a bomb in her mouth today.

He looks at the sunlit hole in the ceiling with his eyes squinted. 'Not much – I like to be cool.'

It is cool. It's a relief to be in this place. When she's here she sits differently – her arms slumped by her sides and her legs sticking straight out. She kicks off her shoes and lets the flagstones chill her feet.

At home, the sweet ripeness still in her mouth, she finds Marc already there, back from work. He fusses around in the open-plan kitchen of their apartment making green tea.

'You're back early?' Her hand flutters on the lock of their front door.

'Yeah. I've got a headache. Munroe, he's being such a pain these days. I can't make head nor tail of him. The Americans, they do everything differently.' Marc's blue eyes are a shade paler than usual.

Nadine lies beside him in the night. He snores, making little puffing sounds. But she's wide awake, watching the shadows on the ceiling. She peels off the covers and sees in the dark her nipples have turned to black. She thinks of Madame G in bed two floors down, right below and imagines herself suspended over the other woman's body, floating over the exact same spot.

It's every day she goes to see Gabriel now but it's puzzling to her why. It isn't sex, she's pretty sure of that; he barely looks at her. Their talk of the old days has no destination; the words mostly just turn lazily in the air. They come to abrupt ends. He doesn't mind her being there, but then he doesn't mind her leaving either. She suspects sometimes he's high, there's a sheen of sweat on his skin, and the room smells sweet and pungent.

At night there's pleasure in running through it, piece by piece: the leaving of the apartment, the walk past the statues, then past the row of shops. The last in the row, a clothes shop. One day the mannequin had been changed: instead of wearing a white jumpsuit and red stilettos, it had on a checked jacket and skirt. It disrupted the routine momentarily, but now the check has become part of it.

She thinks of Gabriel and realises – he is never trying to look inside her like the others. He doesn't care what she has or hasn't done. It's dark enough to hide in there. There is nothing but coolness and cherries and Gabriel's company that demands nothing. It's so simple. You put the fruit in your mouth and it's hard and unyielding. Your teeth bounce against the skin. You pierce it then, with an incisor and make jam with your teeth and suck at the fibres left on the stone, wedged up in the roof of your mouth. You let your feet take up the coolness from the flagstones into your legs like a stem sucking up water. You don't tell your husband where you go every day.

Madame G is so often stationed outside her apartment door now you'd think she was a sentry there. Nadine, winding down the circle of stairs has started to hold her breath as she nears the third-floor apartment, hoping her neighbour won't be waiting. Nearly always she is – polishing the door handle, scrubbing the step, or more often these days, simply planted – no excuse.

'I think Madame G hears me leaving, and comes out of her apartment to watch me come down the stairs,' she tells Marc.

'Why would she want to do that?' Marc is reading a newspaper after dinner and looks over it at her now.

'I don't know why she does it. I just know she does.'

'She's lonely. You should try and make friends with her, she's been lonely since her husband was lost at sea. You could do with some friends.'

Nadine wonders if she herself is drowning. In thick syrupy stuff that the air between objects and people is made up of. Madame G doesn't look lonely. She's tight-lipped and suspicious.

'I don't think – that we have much in common.'

He slams his paper down. 'You could at least try. It might do you good.' There's colour rising in his cheeks.

Nadine knows that it's his good job that keeps them in this apartment, but sometimes wonders if the anguish it causes him is worth it. She says: 'Maybe Munroe will leave? Things may change.'

'But we weren't talking about that, we were talking about you. And things won't change.' His skin is tight and pale.

'They might…'

'No Nadine. Nothing changes. Nothing has changed here has it?' He slams his paper down. Then his voice hums with malice: 'You know sometimes, quite often… I think you have no soul. It's like you are made of nothing.'

When she doesn't answer he leaves the flat noisily and she hears his footsteps going round and round, descending the spiral of the staircase. The sun pops below the roofs opposite and the apartment becomes instantly darker.

Perhaps he's right; she's empty even of that. That's why she craves to be entombed each day below the street. Madame G can see it all, that's why she waits to stare. Nadine slides across the bench where they sit to eat. She rests her head in her hands and thinks for a moment she can feel a cherry stone, lodged right in the centre of her brain. The sensation is so strong she shunts the back of her head with a hand. As if this could force it out, squeezing it through her tear duct and for it to plop, jellied with her own matter, onto the dining table. But the feeling is stuck fast; nothing short of cutting open her brain will remove it.

The next day Madame G is not at her post. The door is open and a vacuum cleaner is grinding up and down inside. Relieved, Nadine hurries past. At Gabriel's, she thinks he's gone out at first. The underground room is empty and his chair pushed to one side. But once Nadine's eyes have adjusted to the darkness she sees that the green door is open, and he's standing on the other side.

'You're back.' He sounds vague. 'I just heard the front bell ring in my apartment.'

It's an ordinary hallway on the other side. There's a wooden floor, boots and an umbrella stand. She wants to eat a cherry but holds off, waiting till he returns. She thinks of the red skin and the flesh inside, as dense and succulent as ham.

He clicks the green door shut and comes to sit opposite her, pushing across the plate as usual. But now she just rolls the cherry around in her palm.

'Is something wrong?'

'My apartment is so bright.' She wrinkles her eyes as if she were there now.

'So?'

It comes out in a rush. 'Sometimes I think he can see right

through me. My insides and my brain pulsing away, like one of those jellyfish that wash up on the beach.' She presses the cherry into her skin, making a dent.

'But why would that matter? You've done nothing wrong.'

(Yes you have. You did it to yourself, Nadine.)

He reaches for her hand, unpeels her fingers from their fists. He holds his hand over hers and she feels the nub of the cherry between their palms.

She remembers Madame Cloutier's thin frame stuck in the middle of the classroom.

'She let things leak out, that teacher,' says Nadine. 'That's where she went wrong.

In Marseilles the statues cast funny shadows, they are black, black against the burnt-out ground. In the afternoon people stay in doorways, watching the street from the shade. The smell of skunk hangs in the air and follows you as you walk. It pokes its sultry head down into the cellar but can't be bothered to pursue you there.

A car moves slowly down the street and Arab rap music vibrates the windows. Nadine thinks it could be following her. She passes a couple kissing in a doorway and the noise of it is like fruit being eaten, ripe mangoes.

Then the stumbling into the light afterwards, the cherry juices a red seam round your mouth. On days like this it feels like every dirty cat on the street knows who you are and where you've been. That your husband might find out that you're weak and strange. That you are just breath that weaves between his solid body and

Madame G, up and down, moving between the floors of the apartments.

It's much later than she thought so she has to walk quickly home. Inside, the sun hasn't yet quite slipped below the roofs opposite. It lights up the whole room, shining on the silver and the rows of glasses so they throw their reflections onto the walls in arcs.

It's immediate, the way her eye goes to the bowl of bright cherries on the windowsill. They glisten in the sun like a fresh red heart, torn out in a violent crime. Panic rises up through her body, ending in her throat.

She can hear the shower running, Marc must be home. She tries to reason with herself, he stopped off to buy them – there's probably wine somewhere.

But each one, its stalk upended, is a bomb ready to explode. She senses they've materialised there from the dark cellar beneath the street, as a warning to her husband. She goes right up to them. She'd like to send them tipping into the street below, get rid of them quickly like she would bright, fresh blood in the toilet pan.

She holds out a hand to touch them, because they seem unreal, as if covered with sticky red paint.

Little Judas

Lisa Berry

Dad used to have hair. I know because I saw it in the wedding photos. It was really black and shiny like his shoes and there was loads of it all combed back in this big point, like the Count's off *Sesame Street*. But for as long as I could remember he'd had no hair. Well, he had some but it went sideways across his head instead of all over. He wasn't ill, not like Bernadette Lehane's mum. Mum said that poor cow had to wear a headscarf because she was as bald as a coot on account of a medicine that made her hair fall out after she'd had her womb taken away. Dad was just bald.

Then one night he came home with new hair.

Me and Mum were watching *3-2-1*. I really wanted a Dusty Bin, but Mum said that bin was for losers not winners. She was up one end of the settee, her feet under my bum to keep them warm. The air was thick with smoke from a cigarette burning in the ashtray where she'd forgotten she'd lit it. I was eating Tea of the Week: cheese on toast with brown sauce.

'Fuck me, where'd you get that?' Mum said when Dad walked in the front room. He didn't answer. He didn't answer me either when I asked him why.

The new hair was weird. Dull black, not shiny. There was loads of it like in the wedding photos and it was high and round and swept back and up at the sides like when Mum did her hair with the tongs and it had a big swoopy flick at the front. It was like Dad was doing an impression of himself. And it made the house smell because Dad rubbed a cream on his head when he took the hair off at night. The cream smelt a bit like sick, but also sweet, like Anglo Bubbly. I used to love chewing that stuff; you could blow massive bubbles with it that lasted ages, but I stopped after the new hair arrived. When Dad scratched his head, which he did a lot when he first got it, the hair moved backwards and forwards in one piece. I couldn't take my eyes off it then.

It was better before the new hair. Mum and Dad stopped talking after it arrived. I suppose they didn't talk much before really. When she first showed me her wedding photos, Mum told me I was in them but you couldn't see me because I was in her belly. I felt good about that because I didn't have any pictures of me, Mum and Dad together, so it made the photos extra special. And Mum looked really pretty in them even if she hadn't got married in a big white dress in St Patrick's because Father Jim said she'd committed a mortal sin and couldn't. Mum had loads of hair too, but it was bright like Narnia snow and in a shape called a beehive. Her teeth glowed and her eyes and nails were all sparkly. She looked magical.

But then she said the only reason she got married was because Granddad told her she had to. If she hadn't been in the family way, she would have been able to go to Barbados on a big ship and be a singer. I didn't believe that. For a start, I thought the point of being a grown-up was that you didn't have to do anything unless you wanted to: why have photos taken and smile in them if you *had* to get married? And she still sang, except it was in our front room not on a boat. And, when I thought about it, telling me she only got married because she was pregnant wasn't a kind thing to say. It wasn't as if I'd asked her a question she didn't want to answer, like I usually did. She'd told me for no reason when all I'd been saying was how pretty she looked.

It was Dad who stopped talking to Mum really because she kept laughing at his new hair. Not laughing happy, but like Nadine Brown did when she told me I smelt of cheese. I didn't laugh at Dad. I thought he was a bit brave because he acted just the same as when he was bald the first time Big Nan and Granddad saw his new hair, even though they kept talking to it instead of to him. I wondered what the men he worked with down the bus garage said about it.

I hated my hair because it was bright red and curly, but I also hated having it cut because Mum did it really badly and she always took loads off so she didn't have to do it very often. The worst thing ever was if she cut my hair on a Friday night because then I had to wait until Monday before the others saw it. That ruined the whole weekend. I knew that before I'd even got through the school gates Nadine Brown and her lot would start and wouldn't shut up all day until they'd made me cry or hit one of them: 'Does your Mum close her eyes when she cuts your hair, Veronica Maloney? Does your ginger hair smell cos you wash it with lard, Veronica Maloney?' I wondered what they'd say if I did the opposite to Dad and went to school one day with no hair. That made me laugh out loud. I imagined walking past them with a big smile on my face and them staring at me with their mouths opening and closing with no words coming out for once, only air. I liked that.

Big Nan was round ours more after the new hair arrived, not just on weekends. When she was there Mum told me to go and play in my bedroom because they were 'talking'. There was no point listening at the top of the stairs or creeping back down them either because she always caught me. In my bedroom I traced my finger over the clowns' big red smiling mouths on the wallpaper. Mum said I was too old for it but I'd helped Dad put the paper up and I wanted to keep it. I wished I was in the circus with the clowns, having fun. Away from everything. Then I started picking my nose and wiping the bogeys on their orange wigs. It made me sad but I couldn't stop.

Auntie Pat stopped coming round though. She was Big Nan's daughter like Mum was. She looked like Mum except her face was more creased. And she wore a massive long white fur coat in the winter and smoked her cigarettes in a holder like Cruella De Vil off *One Hundred and One Dalmatians*. She wasn't evil like Cruella though. I liked Auntie Pat because she always threw her big coat around me and hugged me into her, tight, like she meant it. She smelt like the best sweet ever and I never wanted to let her go. And she'd always had a good eye for a meal ticket, according to Mum. I wondered if that was why Auntie Pat worked down the Wimpy bar.

There were no more parties either. For as long as I could remember, Granddad, Big Nan and Auntie Pat used to come round ours on weekends. Uncle Terry never came with her on account of him being self-conscious about his withered hand in company, Auntie Pat said. We had a bar under the stairs, in the shape of a half moon and made of squishy black pretend leather with white plastic twirly stools. I liked to sit on a stool in my nightie and watch Dad do the drinks for everyone. Port and lemon for Big Nan, stout for Granddad, Cinzano and lemonade for Mum and Auntie Pat, pale ale for Dad and cream soda and a bag of Salt 'n' Shake for me. I'd have my drink, eat my crisps and spin round for a bit until I felt sick and had to stop. It felt good on the stool though.

After a while Mum always told me I should be in bed but I just went to the top of the stairs and sat there until I fell asleep. I knew that once she put the record player on and started singing she wouldn't notice I was still up. Mum forgot to be angry when she sang. I liked that. 'You'd think Karen Carpenter herself was in the room,' Big Nan said. Then Dad would be Neil Diamond and Auntie Pat'd be Barbra Streisand. Then Granddad would sing a song to Big Nan called *I'll Take You Home Again, Kathleen*, even though her name was Mo, and Big Nan would tell him he was making a holy show of himself even though you could tell she liked it really.

But one party night after the new hair arrived, I woke up on the stairs to arguing not singing. Granddad and Big Nan were sort of pushing Auntie Pat out of the front door and Mum was shouting after her: 'Don't you ever show your face round here again. You're no fucking good; I should know that by now.' Then Auntie Pat laughed in this snorty way and said: 'That's rich, coming from you.' Then Mum said: 'Coming from me? You fuc–.' Then Dad slammed the door and Mum started screaming at him. Then it went quiet.

Next day I asked Mum why Auntie Pat was no good and she shut me in the coal bunker for a bit, but not before she'd wet-slapped me hard on the legs and said: 'Little girls should be seen and not heard.' That was really stupid because she couldn't see me in there could she, but she could hear me shouting to be let out.

After the parties stopped Mum went to bed early, Dad went out and I watched *Play Your Cards Right*. I missed the parties.

There were some good things about the new hair. Dad took me out more, especially at weekends. On the ferry over the Thames to see Nanny Maloney in Silvertown. When the boat set off loads of gulls flew after it, squawking. Dad said it was because all the water was stirred up and they were looking for food. I used to imagine one of those birds swooping down, getting hold of the new hair in its yellow beak and flying off with it to use for a nest and my Dad looking like his bald self again. But it never happened.

Mum called Nanny Maloney a spiteful old cow because she'd asked Dad if he was sure I was his when Mum got pregnant. That's why she wasn't in the wedding photos. But I thought Nanny Maloney couldn't have meant it because she was always kind to me. I liked going to her flat. And I liked her. She was as short as me for a start, which no other grown-up I knew was. And she had loads of curly hair too but hers was the colour of candyfloss. And she never laughed at Dad's new hair. But best of all she had a massive Alsatian called Martha that she got as a guard dog after Granpa Maloney got put in the nuthouse and never came out. She let me take Martha for a walk all on my own while she stayed indoors talking with Dad.

I loved Martha very much. She always wagged her tail when she saw me and gave me a big, slobby lick and let me cuddle her. I didn't feel scared when I was with her. I wished Nadine Brown lived in Silvertown because I bet she wouldn't call me little fatty or laugh at my hair and pink glasses if she saw me with Martha. She wouldn't say anything. She'd just know what it felt like to be frightened for a change.

Nanny Maloney always gave me 20p for sweets when we were going home. She gave Dad money too, but loads more than 20p. Once after we'd been to see her, Dad said he was going to buy some new shoes from Cuffs, a proper shop, not the market where we usually bought them. I held his hand when we walked through the doors. It was big and the floors were all shiny and made of wood.

Dad spent ages trying on different shoes. Twisting his foot this way and that way in the mirror and asking me what I thought without waiting for an answer, just like Mum did. He chose these ones made of pretend pythons. They're massive snakes. I know because I saw one up London Zoo once. It stared at me for ages without moving and kept sticking its tongue out. I was glad the shoes weren't made of real pythons because even though the thought of snakes made me hold my breath until I felt dizzy, it wasn't nice thinking of them ending up on someone's feet. The pretend python shoes were brown and black with goldy bits in them, and a big heel and no laces. I asked Dad if he was going to wear them to work. He laughed but he didn't answer.

When he paid Dad licked his finger and counted each note slowly into the shop man's hand like he wanted everyone to see. I'd never seen so much money. 'Is Nanny Maloney rich, Dad?' I asked. He pretended to laugh and didn't answer again. Instead he said: 'Remember this when you're a grown-up Ronnie: always buy a good pair of shoes and a good bed, because if you're not in one you're in the other. Ain't that right?' He winked at the shop man. I didn't like him because he kept having quick looks at Dad's hair like he thought I couldn't see, with this sort of twisty smile on his face.

For a while Dad took me to the cinema too on Saturday mornings. He always fell asleep, even though he said he was just resting his eyes. I didn't like that in case he never opened them again. So we stopped going.

But best of all Dad took me down the Wimpy loads. I only ever went there on my birthday usually, but Dad started taking me for no reason and he said I could have whatever I wanted, even a Big Bender and chips with loads of salt and vinegar and red sauce from the plastic tomato and a Brown Derby for afters. Once he even took me after school when Marcella Warrington was there for her birthday. I wanted to tell her she could keep her smelly old party, even if Mr Wimpy was at it, because my Dad took me out for my tea even when it wasn't a special day. All I had to do was promise not to tell Mum. That made me feel funny at first but, when I thought about it, if she asked me where I'd been I could just say 'nowhere' or 'that's for me to know and you to find out' like she did. She'd slap me but she wouldn't know my secret.

Auntie Pat always served us if she was working. I felt shy when I saw her again after the fight, but she acted just the same as before it happened. Sometimes her daughter Hazel was there too and Dad and Auntie Pat said we could sit at our own table like grown-ups. I'd rather have sat with Dad. Hazel was two years older than me but she acted younger. She lived across the estate and was my only girl cousin but we didn't play together. She told me once she'd only invited me to one of her birthday parties because she knew I'd buy her a Scooby-Doo Shaker Maker.

'Stop doing that,' I said to Hazel one day after she'd been kicking me hard under the table.

'Doin' what?'

'You know what. Kicking me.'

'I ain't. Your legs are in the way. It's cos they're so fat.'

'They're not in the way; you're doing it on purpose.'

She stuck her tongue out then opened her mouth to show me what she was eating. After a while she started to sing in a baby voice. 'I know somethin' you don't, I know somethin' you don't.'

I tried to ignore her and looked out of the window. There was a lady at the bus stop over the road. Her carrier bag had split open and tins were rolling into the gutter. She was bending down really slowly to pick them up. No one was helping her.

'Oi, Veronica, I'm talkin' to you,' Hazel said.

'What?' I looked at her. There were bubbles of spit at the corners of her mouth.

'I said I know somethin' you don't.'

'No you don't.'

'I do. It's really bad and I know what it is and you don't.'

'Shut up, Hazel, you don't know anything.' I got up and went to tell Dad about the lady.

Even though I didn't like seeing Hazel I liked the Wimpy because Dad smiled and laughed there, which he didn't do indoors after the new hair arrived. His smile reminded me a bit of Martha's when she growled at other dogs because they both had massive pointy teeth at each side of their mouth, but at least he was happy.

And Auntie Pat never laughed at the new hair like Mum did.

And she wasn't scared of it like I was. I know because I saw her touch it once when I was coming back to the table after having a wee. She was sort of smoothing it down with her hand and then she stroked Dad's cheek and he held her hand. That made my tummy go funny. I turned around and went back to the toilet before they saw me.

* * *

Then it was all over. I was on my way home from school one day. Loud music was coming from our maisonette. A pounding feeling started in my ears. Mum only put Shirley Bassey on when she was really angry.

I rang the bell. No answer. I tried again, holding my finger on it for ages, but still no one came. I looked through the front room window. Mum was sitting on the settee, one leg crossed over the other, jiggling her slipper and sucking on a cigarette. I knocked on the glass.

She opened the door but didn't say anything, just went straight back into the front room and sat down. I followed her.

'I was ringing for ages, Mum. Why didn't you let me in?'

She ignored me and started blowing slow smoke-rings.

'Mum?'

I went over to the record player to turn it down but she jumped up and grabbed my arm.

'Oh no you don't you little Judas. Leave it alone.'

Judas? He was really bad.

'What have I told you about emptying your pockets before

you put your clothes in the wash?' She started to open this scrunched up bit of red-and-white paper, but I already knew what it was. A Wimpy serviette. Then she nodded, slowly. My tummy felt sick.

She turned up the volume on the record player even louder, so you couldn't hear the words properly.

'How'd you like that, you bald bastard?' she screamed at the ceiling.

I ran upstairs and into their bedroom. Dad was sitting at the dressing table looking in the mirror and rubbing the cream on his head. The hair was hanging on Mum's statue of Mary and Baby Jesus in the middle of the table. I wished I had the guts to grab it and burn it on the compost heap like Dad said he'd done with my afterbirth when the midwife told him to get rid of it, but I couldn't touch it.

'Dad?'

Silence.

'Dad?'

Nothing.

'Dad, Mum knows. About the Wimpy.'

'Go to your room, Ronnie.'

I didn't go to my room. I couldn't stand the thought of sitting in there with the bogey clowns and my Dad next door and that music playing and Mum thinking I was Judas. I went downstairs and out again, to the playground at the centre of the estate. There were only a few kids about so I sat on a swing.

'Oi,' said a voice behind me.

Hazel. She must have been sitting behind the bins. Her mouth and chin were covered in ice cream.

'What you doing?' she said, sweeping her tongue around her lips.

I ignored her and scraped the toe of my school shoe on the ground. Mum would kill me for scuffing them, but I didn't care anymore.

'Oi, Veronica, you deaf as well as fat?' She kicked my leg then wiped her shoe down my sock.

I looked at her. 'That day in the Wimpy when you said you knew something I didn't. What was it?'

'I ain't tellin'.'

'Please.'

'Nah.' She shook her head and put her hands on her hips.

'Please, Hazel, you said it was really bad and you knew what it was.'

'It is and I do.'

'Please tell me.'

'All right. But you gotta pay me first. Enough for a screwball.'

I only had 10p. She still took it.

'I can't remember.'

'Yes you can.' Hot snot tears.

'I can't.' She flipped the coin and put it in her pocket. 'Ain't my fault if I can't remember everythin', is it? I've got special educational needs. Wot you cryin' for, you baby?'

She circled her arms to take in the flats around us. 'Look everyone, there's a big baby cryin' on the swings. Ha ha ha ha ha.' She started clapping, fast. '*Cry baby buntin', Daddy's gone a-huntin', Gone to get a rabbit skin, To wrap the baby bun–*'

'Hazel!' Auntie Pat was at the gate to the playground. 'In. Now.'

'*Run, run as fast as you can, You can't catch me, I'm the Gingerbread Man!*' Hazel laughed, climbed over the fence and ran off, still singing.

Auntie Pat walked over to the swings. My heart was beating so fast I thought it would explode out of me and all over her face.

'What's she done to upset you, love? Don't cry, it's all right,' she said. She stroked my cheek then went to hug me.

My tummy turned inside out and back again, like it did on the Scenic Railway at Dreamland, except this time it wasn't because I was excited.

'I'm sorry Auntie Pat, I've got to go.' I jumped off the swing and walked out of the playground. I held my breath until I saw black dots in front of my eyes and the sound went all swooshy-swirly, like when you held a big shell against your ear, but more faraway.

The music had stopped but clothes were falling from the sky when I turned the corner to ours: Dad's shirts, trousers, Y-fronts and socks. Mum was throwing them out of the bedroom window and shouting.

'Go on, you can have all the knickerfuckinbocker glories you like now, you dirty bastard. And take this with you n'all.'

Dad's hair came out. It seemed to take ages to fall, like a black parachute. I felt a bit sorry for it when it landed, all flat and with no head to go on. It didn't look scary anymore.

'Stop it, Mum. Stop it, please,' I said standing under the window.

A few of the neighbours were watching and mumbling, with their arms folded. Kids were turning circles on bikes.

Someone laughed and shouted, 'Go on girl, you tell 'im.'

'Mum!'

She stopped what she was doing and stared at me, her shoulders moving up and down as she breathed. She had this funny sort of blank look on her face, like she'd forgotten who I was. It gave me goosebumps. Then she shook herself like she'd just woken up and disappeared from the window but came back holding the Mary statue. The neighbours sucked in air like they'd had a shock but I knew what was coming and I didn't move.

The statue missed me and broke all over the pavement. Half of Baby Jesus's face landed next to my scuffed shoes.

Our front door was open and the big suitcase was at the bottom of the stairs. Dad was kneeling over it with the fake snake shoes in his hands. He didn't look up.

I stepped over the case and went straight up to my room and shut the door. I sat on the bed for a while with my hands over my ears. Then I stood up and got a corner of the bogey paper, sharp, under my nail. I started to pull it away from the wall in long strips with both hands. I didn't stop until it was all off. I put my nightie and dressing gown in the Snoopy nightdress case Nanny Maloney had given me for Christmas and zipped it up. Then I opened the door.

Lady of the House

Tim Glencross

Annabel is taking a break from attacking the kitchen when she glances out of the window and spies George coming up the drive. The latter wears a demure smile, as though half-imagining the rhododendrons a bank of paparazzi. As usual, Annabel has no choice but to usher her in. About the imminent visit from the food-hygiene inspector, George shows no finer interest or sympathy than Robert; who, however much Annabel tried to convey the horrific enormity of her cleaning and reorganisation task – the guidance she was sent by the Food Standards Authority runs to almost 100 pages – seemed to assume it was the sort of thing his wife rather enjoyed.

Annabel considers this more than a failure of feminine sensibility on George's part: she, as much as Annabel's husband, ought to be aware that the bookshop's new coffee-and-cake area has not been established purely for the amusement value (as Annabel, if she is being honest with herself, may have implied to others). To act as though there were nothing financial at stake if the hygiene inspector denies Annabel license to bake the bookshop's cakes in her kitchen is completely thoughtless of her friend-turned-landlady. The small chance George is actually being rather sensitive to Annabel's nerves, not to mention pride, is dispelled when the former says, with a firmness that's intended to convey approval but also dispense with the subject, 'So it's all going extremely well, the grand *projet*?'

'Oh yes. I mean, not from the point of view of direct sales. It's probably only adding an extra couple of hundred pounds a week.'

George nods vigorously to show she's not frightened of discussing such a trivial sum.

'And of course,' says Annabel, whose embarrassment is buried so deep she barely senses it, 'there was the initial outlay of the redesign of the shop and buying the new Italian coffee machine and these rather sweet wooden chairs and tables from John Lewis. I've had to take on a gap-year girl to be a sort of waitress-stroke-book-unpacker. Then it's all meant quite a lot of extra work for me in terms of baking the cakes.'

'They're delicious, I hear! Everyone is talking about them.'

It's true, Annabel thinks; her cakes have been a tremendous success. Too much so, in a way, as after only three weeks she is reaching the limits of her repertoire and starting to resent customers gushing over her lime-and-coconut sponge or lemon polenta yoghurt cake, before adding they can't wait to find out what she's going to make next. She wonders if this constant competition with oneself is how Robert feels on the golf course; or if it's even the same kind of pleasure-pain that the authors on her (now marginally reduced) shelves experience each time one of their old works is praised.

'The good news,' Annabel says, 'is book sales are up slightly with the extra footfall.'

This is true, the problem being that so many of the visitors to Weald Books comprise Annabel's friends in the village, who come by simply to chat, whether or not Annabel is at the time reordering stock or serving a real customer (in the sense of an actual purchaser) or receiving a visit from a publisher's rep. She always indulges them, since her friends constantly dropping in is part of what she insists makes the bookshop far too much fun to contemplate giving up when asked if she and Robert don't occasionally feel like taking a boat round the Greek islands for a few months, or joining the Padgetts and Bullivants in New Zealand for the winter.

'Fantastic... well done...' says George, who hardly ever visits the bookshop. 'Now, how is Crispin getting on? Such a handsome boy...' she adds, not for the first time, which makes Annabel wonder if a point is being made regarding his other qualities.

'Crispin is fine,' Annabel says quickly. 'Of course, we were all a little sad when he broke up with Lucy' – her pain, in truth, was far keener than Crispin's – 'but I don't think they were really a long-term match.'

'A very elegant girl, I thought. Still,' George says, as if courageously drawing a line under this misfortune. 'Bertie' – the choc-lab raises a quizzical eye – 'will take his mind off things.'

'Actually he's gone to Spain for a while. No, I think it was the right thing to do; he doesn't want to be left moping around in Clapham.'

'Oh? I thought Lucy's father bought the flat for her – on the Northcote Road, wasn't it?'

Annabel flashes a brief acknowledging smile, like a tennis player whose dash to the net has been made to look foolish by her opponent's precision groundstroke. The memory of the woman! Especially as Annabel cannot imagine Lady Reynolds having any firm mental conception of Clapham Junction, let alone actually visiting it (not that Annabel herself ever has the chance to go to

London). 'Yes, of course. I didn't mean moping in Lucy's flat.'

'What's he doing? In Spain?'

'He's studying,' Annabel says, with an air of finality.

'Gosh! You mean a postgraduate sort of thing?'

'Well, yes…'

'A PhD?' George persists.

'Eventually, I suppose. But he's not thinking about that just yet.' It's not strictly a lie. Crispin does have a first degree, albeit after appeal, and he has enrolled in a language school, or claims he has. That course if pursued – admittedly with a zeal that has so far evaded Crispin in all his other endeavours – must lead to some sort of scholarly qualification.

'A doctor…?'

Annabel wonders if George is remembering the long campaign to persuade Crispin to apply to medicine school, or her own tendency to conflate psychology with psychiatry when Crispin was reading the former at Exeter and declaring it his vocation.

'I wish one of my sons was academic like that…'

This is her cue, but Annabel really must get back to sorting out the kitchen. The FSA inspector will be here in less than an hour now. Besides, she really can't stand to hear about either of George's relentlessly celebrated sons – a venture capitalist (a description that eludes George: 'he invests in things, that's all I know') and a filmmaker. Dander or Michael's latest triumph, Annabel realises, is probably the reason for George's visit. She has an awful feeling she read in the *Telegraph* – or possibly the *Mail*, at the dentist's or something – that Dander's consortium's new King's Road nightclub was recently visited by Pippa Middleton.

A moment passes in which George squints at Annabel, who despite her guilt holds firm. 'Now I really must let you get on. It's terribly selfish of me to interrupt you; I suppose I haven't quite gotten over what a treat it is having you on the estate. You'll have to fill me in on what Harriet is up to next time.'

'Harriet recently gave an important address at the London School of Economics,' Annabel announces to George's shoulder blades as they file through to the hall. She's relieved George doesn't ask for further details about the presentation that Harriet, who works in the HR department of a City bank, recently gave at the LSE careers fair. Instead, George casts an approving eye around the exemplary Regency furnishings – rather immodestly, since it was her who chose them. Annabel can't resist closing her palm over the stray golf ball on the table beneath the circular mirror.

'Love to Robert,' George says, eyeing Annabel's closed fist. 'He's up at Knole, is he?'

'No, he's pottering around upstairs somewhere.'

'Oh, he's here?'

George's incredulity grates on Annabel because it is justified, if not wholly authentic. It's so rude of Robert not to say hello.

They step outside the house. 'I do love this Indian summer,' George observes with the matter-of-factness of one accustomed to pleasant surprises. 'Do you know, it's very funny. Roland had a sheikh calling him up. Or the sheikh's representatives anyway. He wanted to buy the house! Can you imagine?'

'This house?' Annabel asks, feeling foolish even as she utters the words.

'No, no, I mean St Claud. The whole estate!'

'Oh!... Well... how absurd!' Annabel exclaims, belatedly joining in the mirth. She wonders if imparting this news was in fact the purpose of the visit, or if it was impromptu retribution for Annabel's bad manners in not asking after George's sons.

'Roland had the impression they were essentially cold-calling, except using Burke's Peerage instead of the phone directory. He thinks it's all completely speculative.'

'I see... Still, what did he say?'

'Who?'

'Roland – to the sheikh's people?'

George folds her twiggish arms. When Crispin was 11 or 12, he developed an obsession with the haka, the New Zealand rugby team's war dance; Annabel seems to remember it involved a baring of elbows. 'He said no, of course!' she laughs. 'Anyway, look, good luck with the inspection...'

Lady Reynolds takes a couple of steps down the gravel drive, the start of a not insignificant walk back to St Claud Hall. She turns and gives a little regal salute. 'I'm so glad the family is in such good shape.'

Get to Know Your Husband in Five Easy Steps

Emily Simpson

1. Ask him questions

What are you thinking?

He breathes sluggishly beside you, his head half-embedded in the pillow.

That I'd like to sleep, he mumbles, eyes shut tight.

You know the timing is off but you're still irritated by his answer. There will never be a good moment to have a proper conversation, nothing more to talk about than the kids' uniforms, or what you want to watch on the telly. The words you share are tiny bursts of irrelevance, dissolving into air, day in, day out.

You roll onto your side and watch the night gnaw at the window.

The next day is Saturday. You try again. The girls are on the sofa, fighting over the iPad. He's reading the paper, perched at the kitchen island. You take his hand and pull him outside, where the chill in the air takes root in the back of your throat, the wind lifting the silly skirt you've worn just for him.

What is it? He asks, rubbing at his bare arms.

You raise your hand to his face, smooth out his puckered brow.

Do you miss me? you ask him.

His frown returns. *Oh don't start with that. Not today. I can't be doing with it.*

He pecks you on the head. *Don't be silly, okay?* He waits for your smile, his foot already on the kitchen step. You give in, cheek muscles straining, closing off the conversation with a blink. You know when to drop things; nagging no longer has any effect on either of you.

Coming in? he asks. *It's freezing.*

He doesn't wait.

2. Read his phone

He sleeps with his phone beneath his pillow. This is normal, you think. Easy to reach when the alarm goes off. You've never seen him be protective over it, but, then again, have you ever asked to see it?

You let your imagination breed. He's sending filthy messages to a woman from work, obscenities about how he wants to have her, what pictures he wants her to send him. He gets hard at his desk, the minute a text comes through. He's disappointed when it's only from you, asking him to buy milk on the way home.

You hear him turn on the shower and you run into the bedroom, fumbling for the phone in his jacket pocket until it's there, solid in your hand. You stare at it.

There's still time to change your mind.

And then your hands devour the keys, hunting for the messages. You hear the shrill cry of one of the kids downstairs and pretend you haven't. You need to do this now; have to know that you're right, that you are unattractive and unwanted and your marriage has unravelled past all hope.

But there is nothing incriminating. You check the sent items, the archive, all of the inbox. There are only texts from you, from his sister, from friends you both know.

No suggestive messages, no kisses, no winks. No pictures of breasts pushed against the screen like pressed flowers.

You replace the phone in his pocket and go into the bathroom, the steam warm on your already-flushed cheeks. There he is, naked and spindly limbed, soaping up his armpits; a monkey dance. You smile. He's innocent. You consider joining him, but the kids are still shrieking downstairs.

Tonight, you will make this up to him.

3. Check his emails

You meet a friend for lunch, a blissful hour of freedom and adulthood. She drinks wine, unfazed by the fact she has to go back to work soon. You sip sparkling water, certain any alcohol in the day would send you straight to sleep.

She's talking about all the responses she's had to her online dating profile. She's gleaming; leaning back in her chair, languidly eyeing every man in her viewpoint.

You get some dirty ones though, she says, amused. *Really hilarious stuff. 'I want to plough you from behind.' Perverts. Bet most of them are married.*

Married!

You are only half-there; instead, you imagine you are wherever he is, hunched over a computer, the anonymous sex pest. You are invading chat rooms and porn sites, screwing these women with words you barely know the meaning of. There are no kids or wives or instructions beyond the screen. Just you, and your irrefutable desire to be free.

Are you okay? Your friend asks, leaning towards you. *You look so pale.*

He hasn't signed out of Facebook, he knows you never use the computer. You can feel the intrigue gushing through your body as you load up his profile. The picture on his homepage is from Greece, years ago. He looks tanned and relaxed, flicking water towards the camera as he runs out the sea. You remember this holiday, it was just months before you fell pregnant with your first. You still had your bellybutton pierced, you could still fit into the jeans you wore at uni. You wince with longing.

Straight to the messages and your eyes scour the list of names, dizzy with a sweet kind of anticipation.

He has messaged a few women. Some from work, talking about work. Some from his old school, innocent catch-ups. But there's nothing concrete here. It's all tame.

You go to his recent activity. He has 'liked' a photo of a woman from work, one of the women he's messaged. *Melissa.* She's on some kind of hen do, wearing a slutty Snow White costume, apple poised to her lips. She's not particularly attractive, but she's slim, and her legs look long and defined. And she's young. So very young. You quickly go back to their conversation, knowing before you reopen the message that he was the one to instigate the whole thing.

But he wasn't. It was just a group message she'd sent about a colleague's fortieth. He hadn't even replied.

You are absurdly disappointed. There must be something else – something about this *Melissa* you've missed. In his saved files. Or recycle bin. You want another go…

That night you have a bath. He comes in and you automatically bring your knees up to your chest.

How was your day? He asks, offering a smile.

You perk up a little, refreshed by his interest.

Good, you tell him, casually letting your legs part a little, like petals opening.

He looks down at you for a moment, quizzically, and you remember that face from the early years, the face that would trigger hours of fumbling on the sofa, or in the car up a quiet country lane.

This can be saved, you think. You can be young and fun and playful. You open your legs a little wider, letting your fingers dangle into the water.

But he doesn't move, and he looks embarrassed, and he is pretending he hasn't seen what you're doing.

And it's over.

4. Follow him

He covers his tracks with admirable skill. The man is clean, you've got nothing on him. He doesn't work late. He hasn't bought a new car or shaved his head or started wearing Converse.

But it's not right. Something's not right. You have to know what he wants. If it isn't Melissa, it's somebody else.

You Google private investigators and contemplate honeytraps; hiring women to try to seduce him. But it all seems too clinical for your relationship. You loved each other, both cried at your wedding, at the birth of your girls. This isn't how it was supposed to happen.

You arrange for your mother to arrive after he leaves for the pub. She's happy to do it, pleased you are going out for a change. The kids cry and you feel a knot of guilt work its way through your throat, but you swallow it down. You wear your everyday jeans and a black jumper you find at the back of the wardrobe that hides your flab. You blow-dry your hair upside down and put lipstick on for the first time in months. When you look in the mirror you don't recognise yourself.

He is at the bar with Bryan, as he said he would be. He's ordering the drinks, sandwiched between two average-looking women. He doesn't look at them; saving himself for the truly beautiful. At the bar he is energetic and sparkly, at home he feigns exhaustion to avoid helping out with the kids. Here he looks younger, looser, he's laughing and there are no lines on his face; the dimmed lighting obscuring them. At home he is a sad sack, crumpled and worn.

You stand by the door and watch for a moment, sucking in your stomach and your thoughts. Your eyes follow them as they choose a table, close to a group of female students. You clench. You can't stand here all night. They'll see you at some point. You know you won't catch him doing anything anyway, he knows it would get back to you. It doesn't matter if you're here or not. You might as well go home.

Your feet start to move. You walk to their table. His face drains of colour.

What are you doing?

Hi, you say breezily. You kiss Bryan on the cheek.

What are you doing? He repeats.

I thought I'd join you for a quick one, you say.

He exchanges a glance with Bryan. You want to cry.

What are you having? Bryan asks, getting up. You ask for a white wine.

Are you checking up on me? He asks the minute Bryan is gone, and you want to ask him, *why, is there anything I should know?* You stare at one another for a long time, and he looks so angular and angry, and you feel so helpless and hopeless and unanchored.

I'm meeting Trish, just thought I'd drop in first.

Oh, he says. *Sorry.*

Out of the corner of your eye you see a blonde navigating the room; young, breasts bulging out like the curve of a question mark. You are irrationally angry about her being here. You hate him for it. You hate him for what he's thinking about her. You want to scratch his eyes out.

Bryan returns with the drinks and there's an awkward minute or two before they forget you are there and start talking about sport. After ten minutes you say you must dash, and you leave, head held so high your neck hurts.

You take your time and walk home, so your mother doesn't ask any questions.

5. Get him to open up

The final straw. You cannot bear this anymore. You lie beside him, just like always, night in, night out. You can feel the insanity bloom inside you. You are lost in the throes of this now. You can feel your heart palpitating, uncertain of when to beat.

You look down at him sleeping, his mouth open and moist, his breath lightly tainted with onion.

You start to cry for the man he was; you pine for him, for the attention, for the nights of endless whispers and secrets between you.

You have never felt so in the dark.

Tell me what you're thinking! Tell me what you want! Tell me what to do! Tell me who you are screwing, who you want to screw instead of me! Tell me anything!

He snores, softly.

You hold your breath.

It's then that you notice it. The smoke coming out of his mouth, the billows of white curling into the air. You sit bolt upright – is he on fire? Is it a joke? But the smoke continues to circulate. You watch it rise up like ribbon into the air, then fall back down towards you, a fog progressing. It's coming for you. You want to wake him up, you are scared, but there are no words left, no sounds but your heart clogging up your ears.

You scramble up the bed towards the wall, but the smoke grabs you, coiling around your wrists and pulling you onto your back. You cannot move now, and more smoke is pouring out of his mouth – his open mouth, so wide now, so much smoke, you can barely see him anymore. It binds your legs to the bed, and your arms, and your head, and it thickens, and you are entombed by it. You start to call out, but it finds its way to your mouth, clamping you up. You wriggle, hot and afraid, and all the while more and more smoke gushes from his mouth and he continues to snore.

But the smoke isn't smoke, is it? It isn't vapour, or steam or anything you can recognise. There are letters forming from it, 'M's and 'L's and 'S's detaching themselves from the mist. There are words now, you see your name, and *hers*, and others, and the smoke and letters are dancing above you like skywriting.

The words become sentences, thoughts.

His.

You gag. You no longer want to know what he's thinking. You are sorry for what you have done. You trust him, you'd rather not know.

When you shut your eyes the words prise them open, and you begin to read, begin to process what you are seeing amongst the streams of white.

Your husband has thought these things. About you, about the kids, about the women.

There is so much of it, reams of it, stories and conversations and situations. Your eyes sting.

The words furrow into you; your nose, your mouth, your pores. Through your ears and into your mind; these words that cannot be unread. These things that cannot be unknown.

After a while you stop struggling and finally succumb, while beside you his thoughts blow freely into the night, and he sleeps, dreamlessly.

The Barley Child

Theresa Howes

This is the last place God made which is why He never allows the sun to shine on it. I say it's God-forsaken, so He cannot be blamed for the gloom or the damp or the fog that rolls across the ancient hills and grips so hard it can't let go.

They said the war would be over by Christmas; that we'd only have to manage until the men returned, so we tied up our skirts to keep them from dragging the mud, and hitched the horses to the plough as we stooped to sow the land.

Four years was long enough to wait to find those who came back from the trenches came back in parts, half made up of limbs and faces; slow-witted or struck dumb by the terrors of the shells and the rattling guns.

There was only one good man among them; Thomas Powell from Brooke Farm, over Crawl Meadow way. My Tommy from our younger days when we scrambled through hedgerows and tumbled out of trees, overreaching ourselves for the rosiest apples. Grubby-faced with bitten-down nails, the two of us displayed our scabby knees like medals; our bramble scratches our badges of honour.

In those days, me and Tommy were evenly matched. Born in the shadow of the whale-backed hills, the landscape belonged to us and we challenged its cruel nature with our fearless hearts. My limbs were strong and flexible as any boy's, as we charged neck and neck, breathless up the steep and stony paths, sure-footed as the sheep that grazed the purple heather we trod beneath our feet. But as the summers passed and the differences between us grew, Tommy teased me for becoming slower and softer. By the time we were eighteen he was holding my hand and negotiating the rocks for both of us.

It was August 1914 when he was called to war. With his suitcase packed and left waiting at the door, we set off one last time, scavenging whinberries in the lonely, wind-scattered place where witches gather and ghosts roam by moonlight. Together we stood on the ridge of rock that pokes out of the ground like the spine of a sleeping monster, Tommy looking up, his eyes narrowing on the Devil's Chair. 'Do you dare to climb it?' he asked.

I looked at the knuckle of stone, pointing to the sky like a vile accusation, where on the hottest days you could smell the brimstone. 'It's you must be the brave one now, Tommy. It's you must unsettle the Devil.'

And as he climbed, the dark clouds gathered, shrouding the jagged rock as they always do when the Devil himself is in attendance. But I wasn't afraid, because I knew my Tommy was brave enough to tempt the Devil from his seat. And as he reached the highest point, he spread his arms in defiance of the wind and challenged Providence to send the Seven Whistlers to fly above our heads and do their worst.

For precious minutes, we held our breath and waited for those seven birds, said to be the souls of un-baptised children whose presence brings death or misfortune, and when none came we knew we were invincible.

With the storm finally breaking above our heads, we sheltered in the cleft of a rock and shared a whinberry-sweetened kiss. It was then Tommy promised to come back to me once the fighting was done. He'd tempted the Devil from his chair, and the Seven Whistlers had ignored his call. It was enough to tell me Tommy would be true to his word. Tommy would come back safe.

The trenches did nothing to diminish him. Tommy was still broad in the beam and just as handsome when he returned to us four years later, blowing in from France with the first of the winter sleet. Every woman in the village stood up a little straighter in his presence, but my claim was strong and true.

I'd have started with the banns before he'd scraped the trench mud from his fingernails, but Tommy said he needed time. He'd moved from one world of mud and rain to another and the shift had changed him.

Ignoring his pa's demands, he turned against farm work, and each morning of that winter he set off across the tracks worn into the earth by generations of drovers. With shoulders hunched and hands fisted deep inside his pockets, he trudged through the snow, showing no care for the boundaries marked by ancient hoar stones.

Every day, I watched his figure from a distance as he crossed our land, the frosted air settling in a silence around him. 'What's troubling you, my Tommy?' I whispered, but no answer came.

All the while I waited. I gathered about me a nest of ribbons and lace and new white linen and thought of sewing my trousseau until I could stand it no longer. So on that bleak day I left Pa to pulp the bitter turnips for fattening the cows and set out after him.

Despite the slip of the ice, his long strides covered the ground at a rapid pace. Years of working the land alongside Pa had made me strong. I had the stamina of any man, yet I fought to keep up, and Tommy seemed not to hear my breath on the wind as I panted and struggled in his footsteps.

At Cutberry Hollow we passed the witch, caught in the act of shape-shifting, frozen in time as a crouching hare; the stone so white, it shone brighter than the moon at midsummer. She'd enchanted our childhood minds and unravelled our imaginations, but now she failed to draw Tommy's eye and I knew her spell was broken.

I dragged my shawl from my shoulders and knotted it around my head, bracing myself for the wind as Tommy started to climb the bony ridge, where in late summer the whinberries grew. Faltering, he paused for just a moment, and it was then I knew. Something had told him I was following.

Desperate now to catch up, I scrambled along the rocks, forgetful of the ice, until my foot slipped, taking my body down with it. Cursing my carelessness I lifted myself off the ground, too busy brushing the grit from my skirt to hear him.

When I glanced up, he was at my side, reaching out; his fingers closing around my hand. 'Hello, Tommy,' I said, but he didn't answer. I looked into his eyes but he wasn't there. Tommy saw me, just as he must have seen that old standing stone, but he wasn't seeing beyond his own mind. I smiled, trying to summon back my old Tommy but his expression didn't change.

Together we stood on the ridge, his hand still gripping mine and I wondered if he'd ever again have the courage to climb to the highest point, up to the Devil's Chair, to summon those seven whistling birds and challenge our fortune. I wouldn't be the one to goad him. The world had changed and we didn't feel so invincible.

Without warning, a single gunshot echoed from the valley below, fracturing the silence and suddenly Tommy was on his stomach. His hands were over his ears, his right cheek pushed against the icy rock and he was sobbing, his body trembling from the shock of it, and from the memory of something worse that couldn't be shaken off.

It was just Old Swyney, scaring off the rooks in Crooked Field, but Tommy wouldn't have it.

Not until the sky filled with snow and changed from grey to light was I able to move him. Silent now, I led him to the deep cleft in the rock where we'd sheltered as children and where on that August day before the war he'd promised to come back to me.

His eyes were wild and unfocused as they searched every crevice and spider haunt of our shelter. He stroked my cheek and I wondered if he remembered that first and only kiss, our lips stained with the juice of the whinberries we'd picked that afternoon and our breath all the sweeter for it.

His fingers were ice to the touch, his breath a cloud, his lips near frozen, and I knew I had to warm him the only way I could. So I lifted my skirt and allowed him to do the thing we shouldn't have done until after the wedding. And all the while I wished for a new life, defying the Devil and those whistling birds that never came.

Afterwards, he was calmer, his eyes intent upon my face, but whether he saw me or not, I couldn't tell. This was Tommy but not my Tommy from before the war, but after what we'd done he'd be mine forever and there could be no denying it.

Winter gave in to spring. The frozen earth melted and turned to bog as it soaked up the rain and wouldn't let it go. I worked alongside Pa, keeping the cattle dry and fed and when it warmed up we top-dressed the soil ready for drilling. Every part of me ached from the work, but there was no time to think of anything else and so I kept my growing secret to myself, and Tommy didn't show his face on our land again.

Widow Phillips, gossiping on market day, told me he'd kept himself close indoors all through late winter and early spring, until his pa had forced him to help with the lambing. No man could expect to remain idle with the ewes dropping all hours of the day and night.

I had to see him. I had to tell him before my belly grew any rounder and he heard of it from somebody else, and so on the first fine day, I made an excuse and left the house after breakfast, struggling with the unaccustomed warmth of a mild morning and the weight of my secret.

Tommy was thinning a hedge at the farthest end of his pa's land. He straightened up and watched my approach; his shirtsleeves rolled to his elbows, his eyes squinting against the morning light. It didn't take many words. After what had passed between us, he'd guessed what I'd come to say.

'It's a pretty tangle we've got ourselves in,' he said.

'It's nothing a wedding can't put right.'

His eyes scanned the horizon where the sky dropped to meet the hills. 'Everyone will know the baby was made before the vows.'

'Then it'll be a barley child,' I said. 'It won't be the first around here to be known by that name.'

'I used you badly.'

'I was always yours, Tommy.' But as he looked at the clouds, I couldn't be sure he remembered his promise.

Tommy said he'd do his duty by me. Some would say I caught him fair and square. He knew what he was about on the bleak January day as we cowered between the rocks beneath the Devil's Chair. Whether he was in his right mind or not, I'd never know and I'd never be sure he was truly mine. Belonging is more than vows and rings.

After the wedding, Tommy found us a cottage on the edge of the village. I spent my days sewing matinee coats and tiny mittens, counting down the time while he worked his pa's land.

Each night I opened the windows, letting in the dark to breathe the air sweetened by the scent of the freshly ploughed soil. And with my senses all the keener for my sleeplessness, I searched the sky for omens.

The Seven Whistlers. Would they come to augur death, or was it just an old wives' tale? Would the partridges, messengers of the same end, hang about the house? I listened for Old Swyney's dogs barking at the stars but there was nothing, only the whisper of the barn owls beating their wings against the night.

When the pains began, I closed my eyes and prayed, but in a land that God has forsaken, I knew there was nothing to be gained. Tommy heard my cries from the corner of Crooked Field and cowered there until it was over, his screams ringing out for two days and nights across the valley.

The baby, when it finally came, was a wretched creature and small, too small to have caused such agony in the birthing of it.

Tommy stood at the foot of the bed watching the midwife wash her hands. 'We'll call him Owen, after my pa,' he said, with no hint of hope in his voice.

The midwife muttered under her breath. 'You'll have your work cut out to make that one strong.'

I looked at baby Owen, fragile as a ghost in my arms, and didn't know whether to say hello or goodbye.

My body healed, but Owen failed to grow. Weak and struggling for breath, his tiny heart beat like the wings of a dying moth; his skin, pale as eggshell in the morning light, too brittle to caress.

He refused to feed, turning his head from my breast, his mouth set in a determined pout; a shrunken creature, silent in his hunger and sleeplessness, and ancient before his time.

Tommy didn't like to touch him. He said something in his eyes made him nervous. I wanted to say he was wrong, but I could see it too.

The midwife said it was the shedding of so many tears that made my milk dry up. Tears cried because my precious Owen refused to be loved, preferring to stay cold when I could have made him warm.

It was as if he was not of our making. This barley child behaved like a changeling, a stranger who'd stolen into our lives and didn't fit, and determined to punish us for it. Every time I held him, his unblinking eyes seemed to peer into my soul, judging me. But I knew it wasn't poor Owen, but the Devil who was to blame.

It wasn't long before the parson made a visit. He stood by the door, clutching the brim of his hat, the traces of mutton grease still on his lips. He said I must have Owen baptised. Children who die without it are not received into heaven. He looked at Owen, so still in his cradle, and warned me not to wait too long. For once he was right and I knew what I had to do.

Old Eustace had made coracles all his life. Beautiful, basket-like boats; curved like a cradle and made cosy with a lining of bullock hide. I asked him to make the smallest one he'd ever built. Being a man of few words, Eustace nodded and nothing more was said.

I walked seven miles with the coracle on my back the day Eustace delivered it. Owen was no burden at all, tied in my shawl, his fingers clawed against my chest. I chose the place carefully, stopping at the point where the river rushes at its wildest, where the salmon leap so high you can reach out and catch them, and peeling Owen from my body I laid him in the coracle.

He looked up at me without expression as I offered him up. His tiny slit of a mouth, too knowing for an innocent, barely quivered. He must have felt the rush of air on his face, the ripple of water as the river took him, but still he didn't cry, my poor barley child.

Standing on the bank I watched the tiny basket tumble in the current, and waited until the shadows lengthened and faded in the dusk, until there was nothing more to see.

When I turned to leave, there was Tommy in the distance, his face as expressionless as baby Owen's; his eyes empty and unseeing, just as they'd been since he returned from the war. And as he approached, I wondered, just for a moment, I wondered if the old

Tommy would now come back to me.

Every evening, we sit beside the fire and listen to the song of the larks as they fly overhead. If only I could count them. Would there be seven birds circling and whistling? Seven un-baptised souls auguring the worst. Or are there only six birds, searching for that other lost soul in the dusk?

Stupid Cow

Ivan Salcedo

Delilah's fingers danced a sultry rumba as she waited for the sound of the diesel engine to fade into the distance. She bit her lip, scared of betraying herself.

'There's a cow in the garden—'

There was no response. She tried again, louder.

'Don't be ridiculous. The nearest farm must be ten miles away, you stupid woman.'

Delilah's shoulders pinched together and the rumba slowed to a waltz. She sighed and peeled her marigolds off with a satisfying snap. She threw them in the bin. She wouldn't be needing them again.

'I'm telling you, Derek, there's a cow in the garden.' She struggled to keep her tone even. 'As plain as day. And it's making a right mess of your prize petunias.'

'What?'

She pictured the scene. Derek's head turtling up from his beloved Austin Reed cardigan (1984 catalogue, page 19, brown with camel detailing; three identical versions ordered that he still fitted into 30 years later, as he'd pointed out to her – she did have a tendency to forget these things – just this morning). The newspaper would have been the first casualty, spoiling the crease she'd ironed just two hours ago. It would be too much to hope he'd spilt his tea.

Derek covered the distance from the lounge to the kitchen

with a speed that belied his age and medical history. He barged his wife out of his way and leaned on tiptoe towards the window. Delilah, wiser and taller, did not need to look again. She suppressed a giggle.

'There's a bloody cow in the garden.'

'I told—'

'A cow. In our garden!'

'—You. But you didn't believe me. As usual.'

'What's it doing?'

Delilah looked up from the book she had slipped from her housecoat pocket. *Following orders, I expect*, she wanted to say.

'Looks like it's asleep. Right on top of... what did you call that one? Ruby or Patricia, wasn't it?'

'Nora,' Derek said, quietly, steadying himself on the worktop.

'Ah yes, Nora. Was that one of her middle names?'

Derek shot her a look. 'What *are* you doing? What's this?' He ripped the book from her hand. '*Learn Patagonian in 21 Days*. Not this again...'

'Learning is good for my nerves—' she lied.

'Not now, Delilah. There's a time and a place for your nonsense, and this isn't it.'

She snatched the book back from him.

'It never is.'

Derek turned his attention back to the window.

'So. What are we going to do about it?'

'*We*? What's this "we"? You're the man of the house, so you keep telling me. What are *you* going to do about it?'

Derek marched over to the telephone. His fingers tracked

down the speed-dial list sellotaped to the handset; 1 – Mother (RIP), 2 – Dr Marshall, 3 – Dr Patel, 4 – Boots Customer Services, 5 – Snooper Norman. He pressed the fifth button.

Twenty seconds later he slammed the handset down in disgust.

'What's the bloody point of Norman if he's never there? I bet he'd have answered if I'd parked an inch across one of his precious lines...'

Delilah flicked her nail across the corner of the book, feeling the pages give a little. 'Perhaps he doesn't think a cow in our garden is an emergency.'

Derek flexed his fingers, and drew them into two bony fists.

'Delilah. There's a bovine quadruped in our front garden eating my *petunia tweedia*. Of course it's an emergency. What else could it be?'

'Oh, I don't know,' she said, innocently. 'A message?'

He glared at her, and stomped out into the corridor. She went after him.

'What are you going to do?'

'I thought I'd reason with it. What do you think I'm going to do? I'm going to get rid of it.'

She studied him as he searched for something in the hall cupboard. Strands of his combover were dangling free, his cheeks were flushed and beads of sweat were accumulating in the furrows in his brow. For one delicious moment she imagined pushing him into the cupboard and locking him in. But then she'd spoil the surprise. He'd spoilt enough of hers.

'Shouldn't you call someone?' She coiled a finger around her pearls, twisting, twisting, twisting. 'I don't know, the RSPCA or a vet or someone—'

He grunted, triumphant, and barged her out of the way again.

'—Qualified,' she said, flattening herself against the wall.

'This'll do,' he said, blowing the dust off an old wooden tennis racket.

'Oh! I thought we'd thrown those away.' A frown flickered across her face. 'Do you remember? We used to play with Doug and Denise. The four 'Ds.'

His expression softened as he thumbed the scuffed edges of the racket. He walked to the front door, making a couple of practice swings.

She followed him back to the kitchen.

'Why *did* we stop seeing them? Oh yes. You got really cross when Doug bought one of those carbon-fibre rackets. What did you call him?'

Derek jabbed his finger at her. 'Doug Ferndale is a bloody cheat and a disgrace to the Tennis Club. I'm not surprised his wife left him.'

She flushed. The 1986 Tennis Club Summer Barbecue. A gloriously hot day. Derek had left early, incensed at not being re-elected to the Club Committee. Doug, dapper as ever in his regulation whites. A smile, three piña coladas and a steel drum band. That's all it had taken. It had felt like being on holiday. A very short holiday.

She blinked away the memory. It wasn't something she wanted to remember, today of all days. His left hand was on the door handle, his right arm holding the racket aloft like a club.

'Be careful,' she said, surprised to find she meant it.

He snorted.

'It's a cow. I think I can handle *a stupid cow*. After all, I've been...'

He didn't finish, but the expression hung in the air between them. He stared at her, seemingly daring her to say something. They would have laughed it off, many moons ago. She let it go, making a big thing of looking at the animal over his shoulder.

'It's quite a big cow. What if you make it angry? It might—'

Stab you in the lounge with a knitting needle, set fire to your blessed cardigans, strangle you with the marigolds, bash you with your beloved iron, or poison you with some 'haven't you learnt anything from Mother' cooking?'. Her mental list was expanding through enduring endless repeats of *Midsomer Murders* – one of the few programmes they still watched together.

'—Squash you,' she said, softly. There, she'd let herself down again. The moment had passed, for now.

The racket dropped slowly to hang by his side. The door remained unopened. He blinked at her, confused. For one agonising moment he looked as though he was going to reach for her hand.

'Plan B,' he said. He handed her the racket and stepped past her.

She rested her forehead against the cool glass of the back door. 'Hello you,' she said to the cow, and her breath fogged the window. 'You'd have told him, wouldn't you? You're not a silly cow.'

She heard him on the stairs, then the floorboards creaked above her head. He was in their bedroom.

A white object sailed through the air and landed about five feet away from the animal, which ignored it. It was swiftly followed by another. Then two blue objects, similar in shape and size. She frowned as she realised what he was doing.

Pair after pair of shoes were decanted from the shelves in the cupboard in the spare room, through the bedroom window and into the general vicinity of the cow. The cow's tail swished if one or other of a pair connected, but it appeared entirely disinterested in the shower of footwear.

'Derek? I don't think—'

'—The cow has any sense of fashion,' she whispered to herself. She giggled. Stupid man. He swore loudly and resumed his attack.

She looked a bit closer at the shoes littering their back garden. Her smile faded. They were all hers. The little shit was using her shoes, and none of his. She pictured the scene. He'd even have to reach over his to get to hers.

As long as he didn't think of throwing…

'Derek! What do you think you're doing?'

She climbed the stairs faster than at any time since their honeymoon. She arrived in the bedroom just in time to see a familiar pair of silk-covered shoes sail out of the window.

'Derek! No!' she screamed. It was her turn to lean out of the window. The cow had finally been coaxed to stand up. A cumbersome beast, well-known for its digestive habits, it had managed to step or defecate on more than half her collection, including her favourite, most expensive shoes.

'You bastard!'

He looked at her, nonplussed. 'They're just shoes, Delilah. It's not like you haven't got dozens of them.'

'They were *my— shoes*, Derek.' Her dancing shoes. Her raison d'être. Her ticket out. Who would dance with a girl with cow shit on her shoes? The stink would never come out. She knew. However much sandalwood cologne Pablo splashed on, he always wore an undernote of eau de ferme.

'A woman can never have too many shoes – that's what they say, isn't it? Rubbish. You've been spending my money on fripperies for years. You can spare a few shoes.'

He held up her last remaining pair of slingbacks and bent the shoe back. 'Besides. More flexible. Longer heel. Better weapon.'

'I see,' she said, ice forming in her veins. 'Like that is it?'

'I think it's getting the message. It'll go on the next one,' he said. 'I'm sure of it. Have you got anything else?'

'You're enjoying this—'

She looked at him then around their room, at the furniture inherited from his mother, covered in endless knicknacks, sorry, family heirlooms. It gave her courage. 'Well, I know just the thing.'

'Good, good. Look – it's moving already. We'll have it on to number eight's garden in no time. Maybe it'll eat some of his horrible nasturtiums.'

She found what she wanted quickly, and hauled it upstairs. The look of panic on his face was a momentary delight.

'You're not serious!'

'Oh, I'm deadly serious,' said Delilah, as she pulled out a golf club from its pompom sheath.

'Put them down, you stupid woman, you'll damage them.'

She held it high above her head.

'Or hurt yourself,' he added, hurriedly, as he took a pace back from the window.

'Derek—' she said, as she threw the club out of the window. She reached for another. 'Have you ever loved me?'

'Not the one iron!'

'It was a simple question—'

He turned to face her. He was out of breath, eyes a little glossy. He looked more than a little bovine, she thought. She sensed he was torn between trying to snatch the club away from her and wanting to see what abominations the cow might be performing to his pitching wedge. 'Derek. I'm serious.'

'Delilah. Do you mind? There are more important things…'

'Have. You. Ever. Loved. Me?'

He hesitated.

She swung the club inexpertly over her head and brought it crashing down on a pair of Toby jugs.

'Christ!'

The gurning remains of Maggie Thatcher and Winston Churchill in clay form leered up at them from the carpet.

She giggled. She'd gone too far. He snatched a club from the bag and wafted it in her direction.

'You've asked for it now Delilah.'

She felt wild, exhilarated. She could hear the pasodoble throbbing in her ears, feel Pablo's strong hands around her waist.

'You haven't got the balls, Derek.'

'You've pushed me too far this time Delilah.'

Swish, swish. They faced each other across the marital bed.

'I'm leaving you, Derek.'

'What kind of a man would want you?'

She screamed at him, swinging, and struck him on the shoulder.

She overbalanced and fell on the bed.

They both struggled to their feet. His eyes were full of tears. Had she really hurt him? She was past caring.

'And who is he, then? This lover of yours?'

'Pablo. We met ballroom dancing. It's what I've been doing while you've been on your golf club nights. He's from Argentina. Pablo Jones. Runs the llama farm up near Much Wendy—'

'A Falklands-grabbing sheep-worrier?'

'He's Patagonian, actually. They speak a sort of Welsh, you know. Very lyrical, very romantic—'

'Welsh!' he spat and swung the club. The sand wedge made a rather unpleasant sound as it connected with her ear. She collapsed immediately, and blood started seeping on to the carpet.

He had a fearsome headache. He blinked several times, took a deep breath, and closed the window. He wiped the club carefully on the towel hanging on his golf bag. He walked over to her prone body and retrieved the club that had landed underneath her. He cleaned that too, and replaced it in its slot. A thought struck him, and he removed the phrasebook from her pocket.

He flicked through it, and found a business card for the aforementioned P Jones, Llama Importer and Wool Seller. Also, Dairy, Exotic Meat and Eggs.

He glanced at a faded photograph of his mother and heard distant laughter. Determined, he retrieved her engagement ring, given in error to the trollop that was now staining his bedroom carpet.

'Till death us do part,' he said, as he put the ring back in his mother's keepsake box.

He needed an aspirin, and the light was fading fast – there must be a storm brewing. But he had jobs to do. He took the golf clubs back downstairs, stowed them in the hall cupboard and dialled the number on the card.

'Is that the sheep-shagger? It's Derek Wilson. I think you know where I live. You can come and get the stupid cow now.'

She looked into his eyes. They swivelled like marbles, blood foaming at the corner of his mouth. He was mouthing something, fading into nothingness.

She repeated the step a couple of times, bending away from an imaginary dance partner. She'd evaded his swinging club with ease, and used her momentum to bring her club down on to his bald spot with a satisfying thud.

She pulled the wedding band off his finger. He spluttered something that sounded like 'cow'. She placed his rings with hers in her mother-in-law's keepsake box, then bashed it with the blood-spattered club until the shaft had bent and the box was little more than matchsticks.

'There was always one person too many in this marriage,' she hissed, smashing the frame of his favourite photograph. She was *free*!

'Who's the stupid cow now!' she screeched, and swept the remainder of the dressing table contents on to the floor.

'Oh dear. I've made the most dreadful mess,' she said, giggling. She felt a pang of guilt for whoever would clean this up.

'No. To hell with it all.'

Stepping over Derek, she went downstairs to phone her lover.

'Pablo,' she said, 'let's dance.'

Glass House

Sarah Drinkwater

It was a cramped, dirty town, set on the side of a hill, with farting factories and very small terraced houses jumbled together like a bad set of teeth. My father was born with a very bad mouth himself, a constant reminder of where he came from and, even after he'd made his money, moved away and swapped them right out for a blank, clean slate of bright, white ones, they never quite fitted right. On the way to dinner with his fashionable friends, he'd smile to himself in the car mirror as we pulled into the car park so he could practise his new face before leaving me with a doughnut and a carton of apple juice under a blanket on the back seat.

Sometimes I would catch him practising the same look on my mother before she went away for good. She still had her face from the old days, from that dirty town, when she was a poor girl for a poor boy and they'd go dancing in the local working men's club. When doo-wop choruses and soft shoe shuffles came on the radio, she'd dance slowly around the kitchen by herself with a strange smile and tell me small slivers of the past. Sometimes they seemed unlikely, such as the night she met my father, when he walked her home four miles in the opposite direction from where his mum and dad lived, even though he had to get up at six for his shift on the site.

On the rare times that we ever went to her world of silent women and small sips of hot tea, it was an unspoken rule that nobody asked how anyone was, nobody questioned the occasional bruise. I was always quick to quieten, but, when my father began to bring serious men in suits back the house, it became clear that not everybody knew the rules and it became a problem.

'You have a family, Martin?' they would say, indulgently, as they patted me on the head and handed over a bottle of whisky. 'You never said.'

There were holes in how we lived, from the small, ragged one my father kicked in the wooden panelled door to our spare bedroom when my mother locked herself in, to how famous he became behind our backs. When I was sick off school, I'd watch earnest BBC documentaries about new buildings to see if I could catch him giving the television that smile so I could pretend it was for me.

It was a campaign that he began, to make her go, and she hung on through the difficulties, even when the dwindling housekeeping money came through late on the day he first flew to New York and the times she'd get the call from the school when he'd asked his secretary to take me out for ice-cream on the day of an exam. She became weaker and weaker, until the day she upped and left on a rare day when we were both out, leaving two glasses of milk and a short scrawl of accusation on the kitchen table. I forgot to wash the skin of the milk off my face until the next day, and it clung to my face like it, at least, never wanted to leave me.

Once she had gone, the project could begin. I can barely remember where we lived then, as what replaced it was so dazzling, but the house felt as shifty as his first set of teeth. My father kept an overstuffed cushion of an office, full to the brim with papers dating back to his teenage scribbles, and when they would float free of his space, it was often the same doodle. An elongated triangle, constructed of more triangles; I would have thought it was a maths puzzle, except it had windows and pointed up to the sun. He built his Glass House, although it was a more complicated project than even he had imagined, and we were sleeping under plastic sheets for months. I'd stopped going to school by then. I was never much of a person; just his daughter, so it made sense for me to stay at home, especially as his lecture tours, book events and consulting work took him away so much.

The house made him very famous. It won prizes. But the house never took to us; only the boxed-in rooms right at the centre were ever peaceful and even they were unpleasantly hot. I was always told off for sweating too much. The sloping glass walls never stayed unsmeared for long. It was like they were embarrassed of us. The Glass House was full of want; the concrete floor was always ready to be mopped and those metres of glass always, always ready to be shined. My twenties and thirties were spent in service; decades dismissed in a half-sentence.

It crept up on me, not going out much, the way that my weight did. Suddenly, subtly, I was marooned in flesh and fearful of the outdoors. I was even scared to look outside of the house; so many people could see in. Curtains and blinds did not fit the look of the place. One day, I was washing up dishes and singing to myself when I was surprised to hear laughter. A group of architecture students had been sketching the house and even the thought of the pale, round mark on the page that I was, made me stick to the inner rooms for weeks.

I'm not sure what snapped. It wasn't a special day; not my

birthday or a book-publication day or the day our groceries were delivered and I got my weekly conversation. I was cataloguing presents he had been sent by fans and someone from Denmark had sent him a novelty toffee set, the kind that his old town made. Clearly, this fan had done their research. I cracked my teeth on the slab, first, and then saw a very small hammer. My cousin had had one, once, and tapped me on the knee with it, the way doctors do, as a joke and I'd cried. I picked it up and turned it over in my hand. For something so small, it was surprisingly heavy and, before I knew, I was walking out of his study at the very top of the house. I only meant to do one, to see how it felt to break something.

When I tapped the smallest pane, I wasn't prepared for the zschoop it made; the smallest, daintiest noise, like a hummingbird's heart breaking. I had to do another. This time, I wasn't so coy and the smashed glass fell to the ground, startling the birds in the bushes. I began to laugh to myself. Next, I used the hand-carved banister to smash a bigger piece, then worked my way round, finally launching myself through enormous panes with the ecstasy of a church bellringer.

I ran outside, my bare feet leaving a trail of beautiful, bright red across the carpet of tattered glass, and I felt the sun properly on my face for what seemed like the first time, like I'd just understood how to live.

The Ballad of Veuve Clicquot

Annabelle Thorpe

'Champagne?'

He looked down at her, lying naked on the bed and something twisted inside him. He had forgotten to think of her like this, her body slightly arched, one arm behind her head, hair messy across the pillow. She propped herself up, her face still flushed, skin red and risen around the lips. In the darkness, split only by a slim shaft of moonlight slipping through the blinds, she looked young again; no, not young, *free*. The usual taut expression, the sense of her features having carefully been arranged, rather than spontaneously formed, was gone, replaced by a blurred, hazy smile. He twisted the cork slowly, feeling the pressure grow between his thumb and forefinger. Christ she was beautiful.

A soft pop and the champagne surged upwards; he let it fall onto her body, setting the bottle on the night-stand, leaning down to run his tongue over her stomach and on, down to her hips. How long since they had been like this, since *he* had been like this; blissfully free of his mind and the memory that replayed over and over, a little more scratched and jagged each time. They had barely kissed for weeks; he couldn't bear to let her touch him; *I don't deserve it*, he would whisper, *how can you still want me?* Sometimes he begged her to leave him. But that wasn't what she wanted; if they separated, she told him, there would be nothing of her left. It would be as if she had never existed.

He watched her take a sip of the champagne and felt a waft of warm air twist in through the window he had left ajar, in spite of her protestations about mosquitoes. It had been the right decision to come away, from the moment they had arrived at the hotel everything had changed. It had been Mark and Grace's idea, a place they knew, tucked away in the olive groves on a Greek island he'd never even heard of. 'We're going for a long weekend,' Mark had told him, over a pint in the pub, 'and we've booked for you too. And the flights. You need it, you and Julia. Say yes. It's all sorted. All you have to do is say yes.'

And so he had said yes, and Julia had nodded and smiled when he told her. They said yes because they didn't know what else to say; because it was easiest and simplest and neither of them had the strength for anything more. In the run-up to the trip he'd watched Julia come home, each night producing something new from her bag; a bikini, a sun hat, sarong, sun-tan lotion. He knew that a duplicate of each lay in various drawers upstairs but he said nothing, understanding what drove her; that there would be no reminders of their life before.

She was wearing one of her purchases now, a sheer silver slip that clung to her body. He leant in, kissed her hard, trying to recapture the sense of release they had both experienced before he had run down to the pool bar and pulled a bottle of Veuve Clicquot from the fridge. He hadn't signed for it, too impatient to get back to Julia, but in just those few moments the mood had changed. Something cold ran down his spine, a ripple of memories; the cellar, the bottle in his hand, the cold draught of air from the unexpectedly open door. He shivered and as his body shuddered against hers he felt the rigidity of it, like she was literally holding herself together. Without looking, he knew she was trying not to cry. Christ, he wished she would. Sleep was all that was left to them now.

A noise woke him. Within seconds he realised the shouts were his own, that he was sitting upright, heart thudding violently against his chest. A wave of grief swept over him; he'd been with her and she had been laughing, giggling at something he was doing, and as her face began to fade from his mind, tears streamed down his face.

'Sweetheart?' He felt Julia move behind him, her arms slip around his shoulders. 'The dream again?'

He nodded, unable to speak.

'Oh my love. I thought tonight, I thought it was different.'

'It *was*. It was. But... I still don't understand how... Christ, how can you bear me even touching you?'

'Because I love you,' she said, pulling him down towards her. 'Because what happened... I don't blame you. I can't think that way. Without you, there's nothing left of her. I'd have nothing left.' Her body stiffened, even the hand she ran across his chest felt frozen. 'I can't think that way and neither should you.'

But he did. All the time. When he was asleep he dreamt about her and when he was awake, whatever he was doing, the events of that morning constantly played on a loop in a corner of his mind he could never quite look away from. He'd refined it, finessed it so it had become like some twisted pop video; an open door, the creak of a gate, the slap of his trainers on the cellar stairs, her bright-pink sandals flashing against the gravel. Then, just when the tension was becoming unbearable, he would focus on her face; the slight gap between her front teeth, those big violet eyes, the blonde hair held back by a hairband – butterflies, he remembered, yellow and green against the pink band.

And then another face; unremarkable, masculine, hands on the steering wheel. A face in sudden spasm; eyes wide, skin taut across muscles, veins frozen in shock. And then the sound, the sound that always made his stomach convulse; a blunt, dull thud of metal against skin and then nothing, silence, just air, air all around her, and then the second sound, body on tarmac; messed up, bleeding, *broken*.

He placed both palms against his eyes for a second and then pulled back the duvet.

'I'm going to get some coffee. Want to come down with me?'

She looked up at him, eyes full of concern. 'I feel like shit,' she admitted weakly. 'Maybe I'll come down in bit. But I heard them next door just before you woke up, so they'll probably be down there already.'

'Good.' He didn't want to be on his own with the sound. 'Will you be able to go back to sleep?'

She shook her head and pointed to the dressing gown at the end of the bed. 'I think I'll just read on the balcony. Just not quite up to company yet. But I promise I'll be along in half an hour or so.'

'You're not going to believe what's just happened,' Mark said, frowning, as Christopher settled into the chair opposite and helped himself to coffee.

'What?'

'I've just been utterly humiliated by that greasy little oik... you know, Nico, the duty manager?'

Christopher tried not to smile and felt an instant spike of disbelief; how was it possible to lurch from the horror he'd been picturing to amusement at his friend, in the space of a few seconds? He felt despairing suddenly, exhausted by his utter inability to understand either what had happened or the endlessly varying reactions he had to it. He forced himself to focus on Mark's indignant face, flushed pink beneath the Panama. 'What the hell for?'

'Well, apparently, Nico quite understands that when a man is on holiday he kind of "powers down" and thus may overlook things he would never normally forgot. So of course it's not a problem that I took a bottle of Veuve Clicquot from the honesty bar last night and didn't sign for it. He quite understands it was just an oversight and knows I'll understand that he needs to add it to my bar bill, and that doubtless it would have been the first thing I mentioned to him this morning if he hadn't started the conversation first.' Mark shook his head. 'Such a bloody arse.'

'Ah.' Christopher thought back to the night before, remembered the cold champagne running across Julia's naked body.

'Worst thing is, I didn't even have the bottle of fucking Veuve Clicquot. Grace wasn't feeling well, so we just went to bed. Why the fuck he thought it was me that took it I've no idea...'

'Christ, mate, I'm really sorry.' He looked at Mark, hoping he would see the funny side. 'It was me. Julia and I... well, we were having a bit of a night of it... we got a bit, well, you know, it's been a while and we just thought, why not, some champagne... but I didn't want to be too long, to lose the moment, so I didn't bother to sign. I was going to sort it out in the morning.'

'You took it?'

Christopher nodded apologetically. 'But I didn't know you'd get caned for it mate. We don't even look alike. Look, I'll go and tell them now, sort it out...' He pushed his chair back but Mark laughed and gestured at him to sit back down.

'Don't worry, I've paid up. Just buy me a beer later.' He smiled a little awkwardly. 'Actually it's kind of payback. I did the same to you a couple of months back and kept meaning to tell you, or at least give you the money but then... well...'

He tailed off, rubbed the back of his neck, unable to meet Christopher's eyes. The other man took his cue, the one he had learnt to adopt at moments like this; bright, breezy, moving the conversation on. *Away.* 'You did what the same?'

'Pinched a bottle of champagne. Think it was Veuve funnily enough. Out of your fridge.' He ran his fingers through his hair. 'Do you remember the barbecue you had – Dave and Jilly came with that bloody dog of theirs and it kept trying to eat the sausages? Yappy little thing, Scots terrier was it?'

Christopher nodded, wincing at the memory. She had loved that dog, made a fuss of it, fed it pieces of her burger when she thought no one was looking.

'Well anyway, it was late on and Grace suggested a swim. You guys didn't want to go. I think Julia was upstairs putting... well, anyway... I guess we were kind of in the space you two were in last night, bit frisky, kind of up for it. She suggested we skinny-dip, but we might need a bit of Dutch courage. Sunday night, shops closed... so I just nicked the bottle of Veuve out of your fridge. Party was pretty much over, so I didn't think you'd mind...'

Christopher felt his skin begin to prickle; cold nuggets of sweat form on his forehead. 'You took it? You took the bottle of champagne out of the fridge?'

Mark shifted uncomfortably in his chair. 'Um... well, yes. Are you angry? Sorry mate, I mean, I just thought I'd give you the money next time, or replace it... I mean...'

'I knew it. I knew, I fucking *knew* there was another bottle in the fridge.' His voice was rising, he could feel his throat tightening, forcing the air upwards, words smacking into each other as they hurtled out of his mouth. 'I fucking knew it.'

'Chris... look, I didn't think...'

'You didn't think, you *didn't think?*' His voice was too loud; Julia would hear on the terrace above; Grace, guests at the surrounding tables were starting to turn and look. 'Because I'd got it all planned you know, everything sorted, because you have to be organised, particularly when Julia was working. The bag was ready, birthday present wrapped, bottle of water, rabbit was in the day bag, all I had to do was pull the bottle of champagne from the fridge and we were gone. But it wasn't there was it? And I couldn't understand it because I knew there'd been one left from the party and I'd thought good, we can take that to Jake and Stella's birthday, no need to bring another one up...'

He was talking to himself now, barely aware of Mark staring at him, oblivious to the body on the chair on the balcony above, book laid quietly on the table, ears straining to catch every word.

'Stay there a minute sweetheart,' I said, and she was bouncing rabbit along the table you know, like she used to, and she just smiled and I thought she'd just stay there, why would she move? Never occurred to me for a moment that she'd go outside. How many seconds was I gone, Christ probably not a minute... down the stairs, light on, reach for a bottle, light off, back up... 30, 40 seconds.'

Mark's face was ashen. 'God, Chris, I don't know...'

'Don't.' He pushed back his chair, vision swimming, heart thudding. 'Christ, if you hadn't...'

'I'm so sorry.' His voice was barely a whisper. 'But you can't blame me...'

But he was gone, lurching across the terrace and down through the gardens to the sea, walking faster and faster, trying to get away from what he had heard and what it meant and what he knew.

'Just us tonight,' he said, when he found her lying by the pool, hours later. His voice sounded strange, even to him, and he prayed she didn't ask what was wrong. 'I could do with a bit of a break from Mark. Shall we just have dinner on our balcony?'

She looked at him over her sunglasses. He almost jumped; something in her eyes, it was almost as if they were alive again. 'Hoping for a repeat performance of last night?'

He forced himself to smile. 'If my luck's in.'

She laughed. 'We'll see. Mark is looking for you though – Grace has gone to see some old friend of hers who moved out here years ago. Girly dinner apparently. So he's looking for company. Why don't you go and have a snooze; you slept so badly last night.

I'll make the dinner arrangements.'

He ran a hand up her leg; even hours after the conversation with Mark he knew his hands were still shaking. 'OK. Sounds like a good plan.'

He bent in to kiss her and walked back up to the room, suddenly aware of how desperately tired he was. As the door closed he fell onto the bed, not even stopping to slip off his shoes. For once sleep rolled in without the usual film playing in his mind; everything was different now. He was *right*; the champagne had been in the fridge. If Mark hadn't taken it… it wasn't much, it was tangential, but it was strangely comforting.

It was hours later when he woke. Something, some noise had echoed into his dreams; at first he thought it was voices next door, but as he swum up out of sleep there was only silence. He flicked on the light, but there was no sign of Julia. Christopher felt vaguely uneasy; according to his phone it was almost nine, and pitch-dark outside. Where was she?

He crossed the bedroom, opened the door and padded softly down the stairs. The pool bar was deserted; loungers bathed in the milky glow of the moon, a soft hum of chat from the restaurant above. Everything looked locked up for the night; she must be having dinner with Mark. He was just about to walk up the stairs when he noticed something that made his heart lurch a little. The door to the honesty bar was open. Crouching down, he peered inside. A strange, inexplicable fear was starting to creep up his spine as he scanned the bottles, praying it would be there, sandwiched between the Prosecco and the Rioja, just as the bottle had been last night. There was a gap.

Suddenly he heard raised voices coming from above. He turned and saw them instantly, silhouetted against the wall; two bodies, oddly entangled, moving together but disjointedly, unhappily. Before he could call up to them there was a shout, almost a war cry; just as he recognised Julia's voice he saw the bottle glint in the moonlight, heard the smack against the skull and watched, frozen, as Mark jack-knifed over the balcony and fell like a dummy into the moonlit pool below.

Author biographies

Kate Bulpitt

Kate grew up by the seaside before moving to London to study for a Writing and Publishing degree. She spent many years in the film industry, first in London then New York, working in casting on projects such as *Elizabeth*, *United 93* and Robert De Niro's *The Good Shepherd* – not to mention the Spice Girls movie. She dabbled in stand-up comedy and sketch-writing at New York's American Comedy Institute, before returning to the English coast. Now living in Brighton, she has recently finished a dystopian novel, *Purple People*, and is currently working on a handful of other writing projects, including a children's book and a sitcom series.

Julie Nuernberg

Julie hails from Wauwatosa, Wisconsin. After teaching English and yoga to Czech businessmen and driving around Canada in a giant hotdog-shaped car for a processed-meats company, she took the 20-hour bus trip from Chicago to New York with two suitcases and no money. It was there she started working on short stories after taking a writing course at New York University, before leaving the city to complete a Masters in Creative Writing at Nottingham Trent. She currently lives in Lymington with her dog, and is working on a novel about a girl who is accidentally kidnapped by a teenage draft-dodger.

James Hannah

James was named one of the Observer's New Faces of Fiction in January 2015, two months before his debut novel *The A–Z of You and Me* was published by Doubleday – and subsequently longlisted for that year's Desmond Elliott Prize. James has a Master's degree in Beckett Studies from the Beckett International Foundation at Reading University, and has had short stories published in Panurge New Writing, Stand magazine and a Tindal Street Press collection. He divides his time between London and Shropshire, and is currently working on his second novel.

Julia Armfield

Julia grew up in Surrey. After studying English Literature at university, she went on to study for a Masters in Victorian Art, Literature and Culture – culminating in a dissertation on hair, teeth and nails in the Victorian imagination. She has blogged for the British Library, specialising in medical history and amputation, and has had two short plays produced at the Hen and Chickens Theatre in London. Julia is currently working on various projects inspired by a rattlebag of different interests – from Greek myths to the Pre-Raphaelites to terrible 1980s horror films.

Christina Prado

According to family legend, Christina used to read books as a baby – propping them up in her pram and turning the pages with her big toe. She went on to study Drama and Theatre Studies at the University of Kent before going on to work at Hampstead Theatre, English National Opera, Channel 4 and as Paris correspondent for *Plays International*. Her work has been performed at the Edinburgh Fringe, published in T*he Printer's Devil* and broadcast on BBC Radio 4. She is currently working on *That Other Life*, a novel about identity and belonging inspired by her father, the youngest-ever serving Lieutenant in the Republican Army during the Spanish Civil War.

Stephen Jones

After training as a journalist and working as a reporter and sub-editor, Stephen studied for a degree as a mature student and went into teaching. At present he teaches part-time in a London further-education college, working with adults who lack formal qualifications but want to go on to university. He continues to work as a journalist, writing regular articles for *The Times Educational Supplement*. He has recently found representation from a London agent for his contemporary thriller, *The Woman Who Ran*.

Kate Hamer

Kate grew up in Pembrokeshire and after studying Art at university, she went on to work in television for more than ten years – mainly on documentaries. She studied for an MA in creative writing at Aberystwyth University before taking the Curtis Brown Creative novel-writing course, on which she worked on her debut novel *The Girl in the Red Coat*. That novel went on to be published by Faber in February 2015, and has since been shortlisted for the Crime Writers' Association John Creasey (New Blood) Dagger and the Costa First Novel Award. Kate was also named one of the Observer's New Faces of Fiction in January 2015. She lives in Cardiff with her husband.

Lisa Berry

After spending her formative years in London, Lisa went on to study English and History of Art at the University of Kent, before training as a journalist. She is currently the editor of two monthly nursing journals, which provide a rich source of ideas for her writing. The process of growing up is a constant theme in her work, and 'Little Judas' grew out of her fascination with this topic. She lives in Hertfordshire and is working on a novel for young adults, which follows teenage orphan Susann as she deals with love, loss and the need to keep living.

Tim Glencross

Tim Glencross studied Modern Languages at Cambridge University. He then worked as a shadow minister's researcher and speechwriter before qualifying as a lawyer. His debut novel *Barbarians* – a satire about a left-leaning Islington family at the end of the New Labour era – was picked up by Curtis Brown agent Karolina Sutton at the end of the 2011 Novel-Writing Course, and sold to publisher John Murray on the basis of an unfinished manuscript. The novel came out in May 2014 and went on to be named a Huffington Post Book of the Year 2014, as well as shortlisted for the Writers' Guild of Great Britain Best First Novel Award 2014 and the Paddy Power Best Political Fiction Book of the Year 2015. Tim lives in London and is currently working on his second novel.

Emily Simpson

Emily grew up in Worcester. Since studying English Literature at university, she's been on a mini round-the-world trip; lived in Stockholm, London and Oxford; and worked as a copywriter for Skype and TripAdvisor. She also has an MA in Writing from the

University of Warwick, where her work was included in two anthologies. Emily is working on her first novel. She is not yet married (or paranoid), so she thinks of 'Get To Know Your Husband' as advice for her future self.

Theresa Howes

After reading English at university, Theresa went on to study classical acting. Since then, she has worked in all aspects of theatre, from washing showgirls' tights and selling ice creams, to playing overgrown schoolgirls and 19th-century tragic heroines. The idea for her short story 'The Barley Child' came from her love of the brooding Shropshire landscape of her childhood and its ancient folklore, whose influence can still be felt in the small rural communities there. She is currently working on a historical novel set in the West End theatre of the 1880s, inspired by the famous Victorian actor-managers of the day. She lives in London.

Ivan Salcedo

Ivan was born in Franco's Spain and educated in Thatcher's England. His short story 'Stupid Cow' was inspired by a Jasper Fforde quote to write about gorillas being in places they shouldn't be. Cows are funnier. His other writing heroes include Douglas Adams, Jonathan Swift, Jaime Hernandez and Miguel de Cervantes Saavedra. He is currently writing a satirical novel set in an alternate-reality Britain, in which llamas can become DCIs and teaching is a respected profession. It begins, as with all great literature, with the death of a hamster. He lives with his family in West London.

Sarah Drinkwater

A former journalist and vintage clothes buyer, Sarah heads up Campus, Google's East London space for early stage entrepreneurs. She established the UK's first baby-friendly startup school, has interviewed Justin Bieber more than once, and, as well as writing, loves Brutalist architecture, Copenhagen's bike lanes and travel. She graduated with an MA in Renaissance Literature from UCL and lives in East London with her husband.

Annabelle Thorpe

Annabelle grew up on the Sussex coast and, after doing an English and Drama degree, decided to try and forge her two passions – writing and travel – into a career as a travel journalist. After fifteen years working for national broadsheets and magazines, she is still addicted to getting on planes and wrote her debut novel *The People We Were Before* – to be published by Quercus in April 2016 – in between trips. She has recently returned from London to live by the sea, and is currently working on her second novel.

Rufus Purdy (editor)

A former journalist, Rufus's work has been published in *The Times, The Guardian, The Observer, The Financial Times, Condé Nast Traveller* and *The Sunday Times Travel Magazine*, among others. Before becoming Editor at Curtis Brown Creative in 2012, he was editor of *Family Traveller* magazine and – from 2007 and 2009 – edited the Mr & Mrs Smith guidebooks and website. Away from Curtis Brown Creative, he also runs boutique-publishing company Bristlebird Books and is working – very slowly – on a novel of his own.

The Book of Unwritten Rules

For more information on Curtis Brown Creative novel-writing courses, visit www.curtisbrowncreative.co.uk

The Book of Unwritten Rules:
www.thebookofunwrittenrules.com

Printed in Great Britain
by Amazon

35952319R00093